"Jealousy is not an emotion I give in to."

Cass could have bitten her tongue out. She realized with icy clarity that what she'd just said wasn't true.

"I find that strange," Miguel murmured, looking deep into her eyes. "You claim to be an artist."

"I do not claim," she interrupted hotly, "I am."

"An artist?" he queried softly. "A creature of mood, passion and temperament? Denying one of the most fundamental of all emotions?" His eyes narrowed. "To accept that, I would have to believe you have never loved."

"Believe what you like." She turned away, but he caught her arm.

"If you are not in love," his voice was harsh, "why are you engaged?"

"Why are you?" Cass flared back, knowing that this was what had been disturbing her so deeply.

Dana James lives with her husband and three children in a converted barn on the edge of a Cornish village. She has written thrillers, historical romances and doctor-nurse romances but is now concentrating her efforts on writing contemporary romance fiction. In addition to extensive researching, which she adores, the author tries to write for at least four hours every day.

Books by Dana James

HARLEQUIN ROMANCE
2632—DESERT FLOWER
2841—THE MARATI LEGACY

Don't miss any of our special offers. Write to us at the following address for information on our newest releases.

Harlequin Reader Service
901 Fuhrmann Blvd., P.O. Box 1397, Buffalo, NY 14240
Canadian address: P.O. Box 603,
Fort Erie, Ont. L2A 5X3

The Eagle and the Sun

Dana James

Harlequin Books

TORONTO • NEW YORK • LONDON
AMSTERDAM • PARIS • SYDNEY • HAMBURG
STOCKHOLM • ATHENS • TOKYO • MILAN

Original hardcover edition published in 1987
by Mills & Boon Limited

ISBN 0-373-02872-5

Harlequin Romance first edition November 1987

CHAPTER ONE

A WARM breeze, carrying on it the scent of chilli and hot coffee, ruffled Cass's hair as she followed Derek's lurching figure from the small ten-seater plane on to the rough concrete.

Oblivious of the limpid-eyed steward's appreciative gaze, she lifted one hand to push her unruly chestnut mane back from her face, automatically reaching out as Derek stumbled.

'Damn it, Cass, stop fussing,' he slurred, shrugging away her offer of help, 'I can manage.'

She withdrew her hand quickly, biting her lip. He had not bothered to lower his voice and several people had looked round. There was no point in saying anything. In this mood he would only use it as an excuse to blame her yet again, and she had had enough for one day.

Anger flared briefly inside her. He should not even be here. She was making the trip in her own time and at her own expense.

Yet what could she have done? He was a director of the Prentice company, and the boss's son. According to him it had been pure chance that the discussions he was to have with Jorge Ibarra concerning the possible purchase of gemstones direct from the Ibarra mines should have coincided with her trip. But Cass had her doubts. It had been a little too opportune. She had a strong suspicion that Matthew Prentice, well aware of his son's plans, had deliberately said nothing, knowing she would have rescheduled her trip rather than face the very situation in which she now found herself.

Hauling his suitcase out of the pile that had been

unloaded on to the oil-streaked landing-strip, Derek
started unsteadily towards the airport building. Small
and shabby, with once-white paint flaking from the
walls, its flat roof bristled with radio antennae.

Cass's cheeks burned as she tried to ignore the
sidelong glances of the other passengers, sympathy
mixed with curiosity and, in one or two cases, a hint of
censure. She picked up her own case and, wishing
fervently that Matthew Prentice had been less indulgent
concerning his only son's fondness for alcohol, she took a
deep, calming breath and went after him.

On the gently curving hillside above the airfield, men
in grubby white shirts and trousers and straw hats
worked among rows of large, spiky plants, hacking off
the leaves with an implement resembling a pointed hoe,
to reveal fleshy roots like white pineapples.

Cotton-wool clouds scudded across a deeply blue sky,
and the air, now that the afternoon rain had passed, was
crystal clear.

Their tickets were checked by a fat, yawning official
in shirtsleeves who, the instant that duty was done,
disappeared through a frosted glass door marked, 'La
Oficina de Información', before anyone could ask him
anything. Derek leaned his elbows on the scarred wood
of the reception counter and clasped his head in his
hands. The rest of the passengers had been borne away
on a tide of laughing, chattering relatives.

'God, I feel lousy,' he muttered. 'I don't know how
these airlines get away with it. No one could call what
they were serving *food*. Anyway, I don't think being a
mile above sea-level agrees with me, and as for that
chicken crate that flew us up from Mexico City . . .' He
broke off and turned towards Cass, his eyes screwed up
against the thumping headache he had complained
about on the plane. 'Where the hell is Ibarra? He was
supposed to be here to meet us.' His hand went to his

stomach. 'I think I've been poisoned.'

Cass set her case down and pressed the bell on the counter-top. She did not hear it ring anywhere. The official had probably disconnected it to prevent it interfering with his siesta.

Had she been alone she would have relaxed and even enjoyed the hiccups that had marked the long journey. After all, they were part of the fun of travelling, provided you weren't in a hurry, and she wasn't.

But Derek's presence and behaviour had built up a tension she had been unable to ignore and found impossible to dispel.

'Not that you give a damn,' he added accusingly.

'That's not true,' Cass countered, her voice quiet. 'But you know as well as I do that neither the food, the plane nor the altitude has anything to do with it.'

'What's that supposed to mean?' He was growing belligerent again.

'Oh, come on, Derek,' Cass was weary of the whole pretence, 'you drank too much, that's all.'

He glared at her, bleary-eyed. 'I see. So now you're a doctor as well. And that's your diagnosis, is it? I'm p——'

'That's enough, Derek,' she interrupted, anger blazing in her hazel eyes. Then, automatically, she tried to smooth over the unpleasantness. 'Look, we're both tired. Our bodies are still on London time. Although it's only four in the afternoon here, it's after midnight back home.'

He glowered at her for a moment, then his gaze fell away and he pushed a shaky hand through his straw-coloured hair, leaving it even more rumpled. 'Sorry,' he muttered, then stared round the unprepossessing room. 'Just how long are we expected to——' The rest of his question was lost beneath the rapidly increasing roar of

an engine and the swish of rotor blades as a helicopter
landed outside.

Leaving Derek holding his head against the noise,
Cass went to the window and looked out.

The helicopter was sleek and immaculate in a pristine
colour-scheme of pale blue and ivory. The pilot's door
opened and a tall, broad-shouldered man wearing a
black, roll-necked sweater and cream slacks which
emphasised the length of powerful legs stepped out.
Ducking his head to avoid the turbulence from the
idling blades, he strode towards the building, irritation
evident in every line of his lithe body.

There was an arrogance about him that tightened
Cass's scalp, making the fine hairs on the back of her
neck prickle. She swallowed the dryness in her throat
and turned away from the window, shaken by her
unprecedented reaction towards a total stranger.

Where could Jorge Ibarra be? How much longer
would they have to wait?

Automatically bending his head as if used to most
doorways being too low for him, the man entered. Dark
eyes beneath wing-like black brows swept over them
both. Cass saw a muscle in the strong jaw flicker and
knew that, fleeting though his scrutiny had been, the
stranger had accurately assessed Derek's condition.

'Mr Prentice, Miss Elliott.' He inclined his head
briefly at each of them in turn and as he looked at her
there was a cold brilliance in his gaze that sent a shiver
down Cass's spine. 'My apologies for keeping you
waiting. The delay was unavoidable.' His voice was deep
and though his English was perfect, a slight sibilance
betrayed his Spanish ancestry. He reached for her case.

'Just a moment,' Cass said sharply, putting out a hand
to stop him.

He straightened up and a wave of heat pricked her

skin as he turned the full force of his impatience on her. 'Well?'

His eyes, so dark they were almost black, bored into hers and she felt a constriction in her chest.

Cass lifted her chin a fraction, determined not to reveal a sudden inexplicable nervousness. She shot Derek a quick, desperate glance, but he was staring at the floor. 'You have the advantage of us, *señor*,' she said with a coolness that surprised her. 'You appear to know who we are. We, however,' frost crisped her tone, 'are not so fortunate. Has Señor Ibarra sent you to collect us?'

Surprise showed for an instant in his face, then his eyes narrowed. 'Apparently I owe you another apology.' The words were directly contradicted by his tone and Cass felt her growing tension writhe like snakes in her stomach.

'I am Miguel Ibarra. You may be sure my father regrets he was unable to welcome you.'

Cass could not fathom the reason for his heavy sarcasm and decided Miguel Ibarra, despite his undoubted good looks, was one of the most boorish and arrogant men she had ever had the misfortune to meet.

He picked up her case and with a courteous gesture which at the same time brooked no argument, indicated that she should precede him.

'I shall look forward to seeing him later then,' she said, leaving him in no doubt that she too regretted him as substitute.

Miguel Ibarra frowned slightly. 'Under the circumstances I think it most unlikely, don't you?'

It was Cass's turn to be puzzled. She turned in the doorway, the pleated skirt of her fawn linen suit swirling gently against her slender legs. 'What circumstances? I don't understand.'

His expression was cold, forbidding. 'You mean it just

slipped your mind that my father is in the Texas Heart Institute awaiting by-pass surgery?'

Cass's mouth opened on a soft gasp. *'What?'*

'And I suppose you are going to tell me you never received my letter asking you to postpone your visit,' he said with biting cynicism.

'But I didn't,' she shook her head in bewilderment, 'I didn't know ...' Her voice tailed off.

He did not reply, merely raising one dark brow. *He did not believe her.*

Before she could utter another word, Derek's voice, sharp with distress, made her look round. 'Cass, I don't feel at all well.'

Her mind was whirling as she focused on him. He did indeed look pale and his features were drawn as if in pain. He was clinging to the counter giving the impression that if he let go he would collapse.

Mentally pushing everything else aside, Cass moved quickly towards him, sliding her arm around his waist and lifting his arm over her shoulder. As he was barely four inches taller than her five-foot-six, she was able to support him without too much difficulty. 'You'll feel better after a lie-down,' she encouraged gently, then looked up to meet Miguel Ibarra's knowing gaze. 'My colleague is not a good traveller,' she said, defying him to doubt her explanation.

'Fiancé,' Derek muttered thickly.

Cass bit back the denial that sprang to her lips. She would not argue with Derek in front of Miguel Ibarra, but that was one more thing that would have to be sorted out once and for all as soon as he was sober.

She hated the derision in the Mexican's eyes, even though her innate honesty forced her to admit it was deserved. How could Derek have disgraced himself so? Had it not occurred to him that it might reflect on her too? Or didn't he care? To arrive drunk on the doorstep of the man with whom one hoped to do business was surely the height of foolishness, not to mention bad manners.

'So it would seem,' Miguel drawled and, scooping up Derek's case as well, strode out, leaving them to follow.

'Señor Ibarra,' Cass was panting slightly under Derek's weight.

He straightened up, turning round from stowing the suitcases.

'It is obvious there has been a dreadful mistake. I can only apologise that you have been inconvenienced. If you would be kind enough to take us to our hotel we will trouble you no further today.'

'You will trouble me tomorrow instead?' he enquired drily.

Cass flushed. 'That is not what I meant.'

'Really?' He made a brief dismissive gesture which made Cass's hackles rise. 'The fact remains, you *are* here, and as a dutiful son I can do no less than my father would have done. You will stay at our house.'

Cass was startled. That was the last thing she had expected. Perhaps he was bound by courtesy to issue the invitation. Well, he needn't worry, she had no intention of accepting it.

'How very kind,' she responded coolly, 'but as you have already pointed out, your father is not here and it was him we came to see. So, much as we appreciate your generous offer,' she allowed her mockery to match his own and was rewarded by a brief flare of warning in his dark eyes, 'we cannot possibly accept.' She swallowed.

Derek's sudden, crushing grip on her fingers made Cass wince, then his knees buckled and as he lurched forward, his arm around her neck dragged her head down towards his. 'What the hell are you doing?' he hissed. 'Accept, for God's sake. Go on, do as I say, I'll explain later.'

'Oh, I think you can.' Miguel Ibarra's voice had a sardonic ring, and Cass wondered if he could have overheard Derek's whispered instruction. Her cheeks burned at the thought. 'Mr Prentice plainly requires rest as soon as possible. The household staff will ensure he has everything he needs.'

Totally bewildered by Derek's behaviour and also by Miguel Ibarra, Cass allowed herself to be relieved of Derek's weight and stood aside while Miguel helped Derek into the helicopter, strapping him into a thick padded seat of gold-coloured woollen material trimmed with pale leather facing the rear of the machine. A brown wool carpet covered the floor and the interior walls and ceiling of the cabin were finished in what looked like cream kid. There was another seat next to Derek's and two more, equally luxurious, facing forward. Cass had never in her life seen anything so patently expensive.

Miguel Ibarra glanced over his shoulder. 'When you're quite ready, Miss Elliott. I do have a few more urgent matters to attend to this afternoon.'

Feeling warmth rise in her cheeks once more, Cass climbed in and sat down in the left-hand seat facing forward. As she sank back against its springy softness, she realised just how tired she was. But she could not afford to relax, not yet. There were too many unanswered questions, too much going on that she didn't understand.

She reached for her seat-belt, but Miguel Ibarra was there before her, deftly fastening the straps across her lap, ignoring or else unaware of the rush of colour on her face at the unexpected and unwelcome nearness.

He had invaded her personal territory and she pressed back against the seat, the faint, spicy tang of his aftershave in her nostrils, aware of the warmth and clean, male smell emanating from him. His skin was the colour of teak and his hair, black as coal, gleamed with health and curled thickly on the roll-neck of his fine wool sweater.

Without even glancing at her he leaned over and slammed the door, then eased through the gap in the seats and slid into the pilot's seat on the right-hand side.

Cass saw him lift the head-set and put it on, and as his left hand reached up to flick switches on the overhead instrument panel, she heard him speak and knew he was talking to air-traffic control. A few moments later the engine note changed, the rotors began to spin faster and, with a barely perceptible jerk, they took off. Despite the fact that the engines were directly above their heads, there was, surprisingly, little noise, which indicated extremely effective sound-proofing.

Cass had never been in a helicopter before. She had never dreamed that they could be so luxurious, and for a few moments she was totally immersed in the novelty of it. But then her gnawing uneasiness returned.

She glanced across at Derek. His head rested against the back of the seat and his eyes were closed. She toyed with the idea of waking him but decided against it. He was in no fit state to answer questions.

Why had he been so set on staying at Jorge Ibarra's house and not at the hotel? For that matter, why should Miguel Ibarra insist on the same thing? His initial reaction had made it clear that they were neither expected nor wanted. According to him, he had tried to put them off coming. But if he *had* written, as he claimed, why had she not received his letter? Derek had certainly made no mention to her either of a postponement of the visit, or Jorge Ibarra's illness. So what exactly was Miguel Ibarra up to?

Shifting her gaze slightly, Cass could see part of his profile and noticed that he had put on dark glasses. As he turned away all she could see was the back of his head yet

suddenly she found herself visualising his face. There
was an almost monumental dignity in the cast of his
features. He had about him an imperial air, all the more
unnerving for being completely without affectation. He
had the curved nose and full, chiselled lips of an Aztec,
yet his broad forehead, high cheekbones and blunt
jawline were all Spaniard.

She recalled the cold brilliance of his gaze, his eyes as
black and hard as obsidian. She shivered, startled and
oddly ashamed at the vividness of her memory.

With a conscious effort to stem her increasing
apprehension, Cass turned her head to look out of the
window.

Below her the Queretaro highlands stretched as far as
she could see. Many of the rolling hills were dun-
coloured, scarred with outcrops of rock and dotted with
stunted trees, bushes and tall cacti. Others were planted
with row upon row of the blue-green plants she had seen
above the airfield. The men moving along the rows in
the white shirts and trousers of field workers resembled
small pale ants. Dust billowed up behind a truck
speeding along a dirt road.

As the helicopter flew lower and banked to the right
Cass saw a cattle ranch with hundreds of black and white
cows penned in corrals munching hay. Then they were
over a valley, the wide bottom of which seemed to ripple
like a vast green lake. Nestling on the far side of the
valley at the foot of another long hill, the city of
Queretaro gleamed white in the sunshine. Cass caught
her breath at the beauty of it. As they flew eastward over
the city, her eyes widened at the sight of a massive yet
incredibly graceful aqueduct whose soaring arches
disappeared into the hills whence it brought water to
both the town and the valley.

She looked across to the other window and was taken

aback to see that Derek's eyes were open and he was watching her.

'Are you feeling better?' There was a touch of acid in her tone.

'A little,' he grudged, rubbing one hand over his stubbly chin.

'Enough to tell me what you are playing at?' She kept her voice low but made no effort to hide her anger.

Derek glanced nervously over his shoulder and put a warning finger to his lips. 'Don't you see? As Ibarra's guests *we* can call the tune.'

'Derek, we *can't* accept his hospitality,' she whispered fiercely. 'For a start, it was his father we had both arranged to see. The fact that he's not here changes everything.'

'I don't see why,' Derek argued. 'In fact as far as I'm concerned it might be better this way. After all, if Miguel is going to be running the show, which he obviously is if his father is that sick, it makes far more sense to deal direct with him.'

'But can't you see that staying in his house, as his guest, while you talk finance blurs the dividing line between business and friendship,' she paused, adding quietly, 'not that Miguel Ibarra seemed particularly friendly.'

'Yes, to *our* advantage,' he hissed. 'Now don't be awkward, Cass. Remember, I take over the company when my father retires next year. You're a good designer, one of the best, nobody knows that better than I. But you are an artist, not a businesswoman. So don't interfere in matters which don't concern you.'

'As I'm being made a party to whatever you have in mind, I think it does concern me.' Cass struggled to contain her anger. 'In fact, it worries me rather a lot. And another thing,' she shot a glance towards the cockpit, 'why did you call yourself my fiancé? You had no right to do that.'

'Don't be angry, Cass,' Derek pleaded. 'You know how I feel about you.'

'Derek, we've been through all this before,' she began hopelessly, but he wasn't listening. He had closed his eyes once more and his head was lolling against the headrest. His complexion was pallid and beads of sweat were forming on his forehead and upper lip.

Cass fervently hoped he wasn't going to be sick. Miguel Ibarra's opinion of them was low enough already. Which made her wonder yet again at his insistence on taking them to his home.

What on earth would Matthew Prentice have thought if he could see them now?

She visualised the short, plump little man who was Derek's father, peering over the half-moon glasses he wore perched on the end of his narrow nose, his mouth pursed as he tutted over some flaw in a gemstone. One of his habits was to smooth with his fingertips the freckled skin on his skull, which was quite bald, save for a fringe of white hair running round the back of his head like a cake frill. Cass had first met him eighteen months previously after coming second in a national design competition sponsored by De Beers. He had written to her expressing interest in her work and inviting her to call and see him.

They had taken to each other at once. He had introduced her to Sam Hart, his chief designer, and Cass had been ecstatic. It had been an exhibition of Sam's work, interpretations of Navajo designs executed in raw silver and turquoise, that had captured Cass's imagination and kindled in her the desire to work with gems and precious metals.

Already fretting under the restrictions imposed on her designs by the firm employing her at that time, she could hardly believe her good fortune when Matthew asked if she would consider working for him. She had leapt at the offer and never regretted the move.

She loved her work, loved the feel and colours of the stones and metals, as with patience and flair she fashioned them into intricate and beautiful items of adornment. Her admiration for Sam was unbounded and he, recognising her talent, had helped it to flower. It had not taken long for one of her designs to catch the eye of a wealthy and discerning young aristocrat searching for a very special gift for his wife to celebrate the birth of their baby son. Now, owning a Prentice ring, necklace or brooch designed by Cassandra Elliott was something of a status symbol.

Matthew had been generous, both in financial and artistic terms, allowing her the freedom to develop. She received frequent overtures from other jewellery manu-facturers offering all kinds of inducements to leave Prentice's, but politely, though firmly, turned them down. Professionally, she had everything she wanted. There was only one cloud on her horizon: Derek.

This trip was to have been an opportunity to put some distance between them, to give herself a breathing space to consider the future. For she knew, whatever her decision, change was inevitable, and there was so much to consider, so much at stake. But nothing had worked out as she planned.

She had been looking forward to a pleasant, peaceful month studying the wildlife and history of Mexico, sketching the wealth of exotic plants, learning the legends and visiting the Indian markets. She had hoped to absorb the essence of a country whose history was written in blood and gold, to distil it later in a series of new designs. Jorge Ibarra had promised her a visit to his opal mines and had advised her to attend a fiesta.

But Jorge was in a Texas hospital fighting for his life. Derek, who had announced his intention of accompanying her only ten days previously, too late for her to change her arrangements, was spinning his own web of intrigue, and all *her* plans lay in fragments.

A gentle bump and the immediate change of engine note brought her out of her reverie. They had landed.

CHAPTER TWO

CASS sat up with a jerk. Still dazed with sleep, she could not remember where she was. Then it all came flooding back: being met at the airport by the impatient, forbidding Miguel Ibarra, the news that his father was ill, and Derek's insistence that they accept Miguel's graceless invitation to stay at the *hacienda*.

She glanced down, fingering in bewilderment the jade velour robe which was all she had on. She was lying on top of the bedclothes, yet some time during the night someone had placed a warm blanket over her while she slept. Who? A shiver pricked her skin as she imagined Miguel Ibarra watching her with those cold dark eyes as she slept. She shook her head, banishing the vision, irritated by her wayward imagination and annoyed at the apprehension and unease the brief image had stirred in her.

Doubtless Consuelo, the housekeeper, or one of the maids had come to see if she needed anything, and instead of waking her, had spread the blanket over her and let her sleep on.

She rubbed her temples. She could remember Miguel leading the way up the wide, curving staircase. He supported Derek while Consuelo, a short, stout woman dressed entirely in black, with grey-streaked hair drawn into a braided knot on the nape of her neck and eyes sharp with curiosity, bustled about fetching clean towels.

Ignoring Cass's half-hearted protests, she had unpacked her case, then vanished to reappear a few minutes later with a mug of hot chocolate. Flavoured with cinnamon and sweetened with honey, it was the most delicious drink Cass had ever tasted. Her open gratitude had surprised and touched the housekeeper whose stony expression had softened into a gratified smile as she muttered '*De nada*, is nothing,' in response to Cass's tentative but heartfelt '*Gracias, es muy bien.*'

After Consuelo had gone, Cass had taken a shower. The white-tiled bathroom had no bath, only a shower-stall, handbasin and toilet, a reminder that in the highlands water was precious and not to be wasted. But there were hot rails for the fluffy towels and the cork tiles on the floor were warm to the feet.

Then, cool and fresh and liberally dusted with honeysuckle-scented talc, she had slipped her robe on once more and returned to her bedroom to lie down for a moment while she decided what to wear for dinner. She remembered nothing more.

Cass looked at her watch. It was six o'clock. She had slept almost twelve hours! What would Miguel Ibarra think of her? She had missed dinner without a word of explanation or apology.

Burying her face in her hands, she groaned. It had been a bad enough start with Derek being drunk and their arrival unexpected and clearly unwelcome. No wonder the housekeeper had been merely polite instead of welcoming. As for Miguel—Cass shivered again, recalling her vivid awareness of him as he strapped her into her seat in the helicopter. An awareness tinged with trepidation. Yet what possible reason could she have for being nervous of him? He was of no importance in her life.

Wide awake now, Cass pushed the blanket aside and slid off the bed. Her bare feet touched the beige short-piled carpet and she glanced round the room, observing her surroundings through eyes no longer clouded by exhaustion and strain. The first rays of the rising sun

filtered through open-weave curtains of green, beige
and gold, illuminating with a soft radiance a picture of
the Virgin and Child hanging on the white-painted wall
opposite the brass bedstead. The heavy carved wardrobe
was clearly antique and the chest of drawers and bedside
cabinet, on which stood a pretty lamp with an onyx base,
revealed their Spanish origins in both shape and size.

Though criss-crossed with massive beams, the wood-
en ceiling was so high it only added to the impression of
airiness and space.

Cass padded to the long window and pushed back the
curtains. In the east soft hues of rose and gold were
fading. Purple shadows melted and the outlines of trees
and hills grew sharper under the harsh brilliance of the
morning sun. Even as she watched, the sky changed
from primrose and pale green to a hard clear blue.

She could bear it no longer. She needed to get out of
the house, to feel the warmth of the sun and smell the
first breath of the new day.

Tossing her robe aside, she pulled on bra and panties
then, opening the double doors of the wardrobe, quickly
scanned the contents. Not that there was much to choose
from. She preferred the feel of natural fibres against her
skin and for simplicity's sake stuck to a colour scheme of
brown, fawn and cream with touches of cinnamon,
emerald or coral for contrast. Thus from a few basic
items she could create many different outfits. As she
wore her clothes with expediency rather than impact in
mind, it never took her long to dress. Within minutes
she had washed and was creeping downstairs clad in a
pair of tan wool pants tucked into matching low-heeled,
calf-length leather boots, an emerald Viyella shirt and a
cream Aran jacket with a shawl collar over which her
hastily brushed hair spilled in heavy waves to her
shoulders.

The huge front door had two enormous bolts. Cass

held her breath, terrified of waking anyone and having to explain her impulsive behaviour, but they slid back without a sound.

Stepping out on to the paved drive in front of the house, she couldn't help smiling as she carefully closed the door behind her. Anyone would have thought she was a criminal trying to steal away unseen. All she wanted was to be alone for a while, to greet the morning and relish the fact that after all the planning and problems, and in spite of the difficulties she knew had to come, she had made it. She was in Mexico!

She strolled past beds of pink, scarlet and white geraniums, over a manicured lawn bordered with flowering shrubs and a profusion of marigolds. The sweet blend of fragrances filled her nostrils as she rested her arms on the wooden railing enclosing a small paddock.

On their arrival the previous day, a mare and her young foal had occupied the paddock, the mare grazing peacefully while her offspring cantered about on long, spindly legs, uttering shrill whinnies and kicking up his tiny heels for the sheer joy of being alive. The paddock was empty now and dew spangled the grass, reflecting the sunlight like a million scattered diamonds.

Cass turned to look at the house. The morning sun had washed the white walls pale gold, and the tiles above the veranda and on the roof were the colour of blood. An ivy-like creeper spilled glossy green leaves over the veranda arches, emphasising the jewel colours of the blooms in terracotta pots resting on the carved balustrade below.

She moved on past the paddock, trailing her fingers lightly over the rough wooden rail, enjoying its texture. She felt wonderfully alive, all her senses finely tuned. The air was cool and fresh on her skin, yet when she lifted her face to the sun, its gentle warmth penetrated her very bones. Among the chirping, twittering birds, she could hear doves cooing. Drawing in a deep, lingering breath, she smelled not only the flowers, but the sweet mustiness of hay and the richness of damp earth.

At the far end of the house she hesitated, glancing into a courtyard surrounded on three sides by buildings. A quick look down the right-hand side revealed six stable doors, all closed except one which was fastened back against the wall. The other sides each had a set of double doors plus a single door in them. Cass guessed they held feed, tack, cleaning equipment and the other paraphernalia connected with horses.

The walls of the stable block were as pristine as those of the main house. The doors were freshly stained and varnished, and stone troughs of flowers stood in the centre of the spotlessly clean yard.

Such care reflected the investment of a great deal of money. Were the horses another of Jorge Ibarra's business interests, Cass mused, or did he keep them purely for pleasure, a hobby, albeit an expensive one, to take his mind off the pressure of work?

Beyond the stable block the ground sloped away down a gentle incline marked by a small stand of oaks. Lost in her thoughts, Cass followed the trail down. The horses had to be Jorge's. She simply could not see his son possessing the necessary patience. He radiated forcefulness and drive and appeared to have his temper on a permanently tight rein.

Enjoying an unaccustomed sense of peace and wellbeing, Cass sighed happily. Maybe she was being unfair. Maybe he'd just had a bad day. Maybe underneath that arrogant, forbidding exterior he was gentle and tender. And maybe pigs flew!

She was aware of an irregular, muffled thudding, but it did not register on her conscious mind until she reached the bottom of the slope and emerged from the trees. The ground opened out into a natural grassy basin and at the far side, roughly fifty feet away, Miguel Ibarra was trying to control a magnificent chestnut stallion whose black mane and tail flew as it plunged and reared.

Cass stood perfectly still, realising that any distracting move on her part could startle the animal into even greater efforts to unseat its rider.

With flattened ears and rolling eyes the horse skittered sideways, tossing its head and, as it jerked and sidled towards her, she could see great dark patches of sweat on its chest and shoulders. Flecks of foam flew from the sides of its mouth as it plunged its head down between stiffened forelegs.

Beneath close-fitting cream breeches, Miguel's thigh muscles tautened as he exerted a steady pressure against the animal's heaving sides. The sleeves of his yellow sweater were pushed half-way up his forearms, exposing sun-browned skin covered with dark hair. He held the reins lightly, his wrists low, restraining the violent movements with gentle firmness as he urged the stallion forward, talking softly and continuously. The deep, soothing tones reached Cass quite clearly on the still air and, although she could not understand what he was saying, the sound was hypnotic.

She wondered what it would be like to be made love to in this liquid, lyrical language. At once a fiery tide flooded her face as she recognised the direction of her thoughts and saw how close Miguel and the horse had come.

She offered a tentative smile, expecting nothing more than a brief 'good morning,' but he passed within a few feet of her without so much as a sideways glance.

Cass was acutely uncomfortable, and the sense of rejection stung like a slap. She felt like an interloper, as

though she had been caught somewhere she had no right
to be. Staring unseeingly at her feet, she tried to
rationalise her feelings. She was over-reacting. He
obviously had his hands full, and the spirited animal,
which was doubtless extremely valuable, required his
full attention.

The stallion had calmed considerably. While it was
still trying to fight the curbing bit, Miguel had coaxed it
into a canter. Its hooves drummed a rhythm on the
coarse grass, muscles bunching beneath the gleaming,
sweat-darkened coat.

Miguel moved as one with the horse, his back straight,
his shiny black boots quite still in the stirrups. As the
stallion finally acknowledged its master, Miguel guided
it into figures-of-eight, forcing it to change the leading
leg at each turn. The stallion responded faultlessly and
Cass felt an unexpected lump in her throat. There was
no victor and vanquished in the battle of wills. Man and
animal had reached a new understanding. Miguel Ibarra
had demanded and received the stallion's obedience
without in any way damaging its spirit.

Instead of swinging into another loop, Miguel
suddenly turned the stallion towards her and, before she
could move, was alongside.

She could feel the stallion's hot breath, see the steam
rising from its glossy flanks. The creak of leather and
jingle of the bit were loud in her ears.

Miguel said nothing as he gazed down at her from the
saddle, apparently waiting for her to speak. He appeared
totally relaxed, yet her one brief glance upward had not
missed the sweat that dewed his forehead and dampened
his thick hair into curls at neck and temple.

'He's magnificent,' she said softly, reaching out to
stroke the stallion's arched neck, aware of the massive
strength beneath the hot, satiny coat. The horse tossed
its head and she talked to it and blew gently into its

nostrils, smoothing the velvety skin of its muzzle.

'You are not afraid of horses?' Miguel sounded mildly surprised. Her hackles rose, but she did not allow her pique to show.

'Why should I be?' she responded, gazing in unfeigned admiration at the stallion's beautifully shaped head. 'I've ridden since I was a child.' She shifted her gaze to find him staring at her, a frown drawing his brows into a thick black line.

'Tomorrow you may accompany me,' he announced with the air of someone conferring a great favour. 'Come to the stables at six and we will ride into the hills to watch the sunrise.' His gaze swept over her. She had no idea what he was thinking. He seemed to have total control over his expression, but Cass's intuition told her he was issuing a challenge which he expected her to turn down.

Pride tilted her chin. 'How could I refuse such a charming invitation.' Her irony was unmistakable and inclining her head briefly, she turned to go.

'How is your fiancé this morning?' His sardonic tone followed her, sliding under her skin like a thorn.

She glanced over her shoulder in time to see him dismount and flip the reins over the stallion's head.

She kept her voice even. 'I wouldn't know. I haven't seen him. And for the record, he's not my fiancé.' She started up the slope, feeling a tightness in her midriff as she realised he was right behind her. The stallion, now rid of its burden, walked placidly beside him.

'That is not the impression I got.'

She stopped and swung round to face him. 'Señor Ibarra, I am not responsible for your *impressions*.'

'Does that mean Mr Prentice will assume the undoubtedly fortunate position of being your fiancé at some time in the future, then?'

'No, it does not,' Cass snapped. 'And I cannot see this is any of your business.' She started walking faster, anxious now to get away, to return to her room. He had brought it all back; the memories, the tension, the arguments. She had wanted to escape them for just a little while. And he had forced her to admit that her decision was made. She had not known herself until she heard the words on her own lips. But she should have told Derek first. She owed him that at least.

'You are a guest in my house, surely I have a right to be concerned?'

'Concerned about what?' Cass flung at him. 'Certainly Derek was under the weather when we arrived, but you need not be *concerned* about that. As I explained, he is a very nervous traveller, he hates flying, so he had a drink to calm him down.'

'Indeed,' Miguel agreed, the downward curve of his mouth indicating his distaste. 'He was certainly very *calm* when I met you. Had he been any *calmer* he would have passed out.' Miguel went on, 'You might warn him when he recovers, the effects of ... travelling ... are far more pronounced at this altitude.'

She swallowed, her reply automatic. 'I can only apologise and assure you that such behaviour is quite out of character.' She flushed under the intentness of his gaze.

'Why do you say that?' he demanded, openly curious. 'You know it is not true. Why do you lie for him?'

Cass gasped, hot with embarrassment at his perception and anger at his impertinence. 'Señor Ibarra, you have just pointed out that I am a guest in your house. A situation, I might add, over which I had no control. But that does not give you the right to ... to ... cross-examine me!'

Her heart thudded against her ribs. She had never spoken like that to anyone. How many times had she bitten her tongue instead of standing up for herself against Derek? Why had she done it? Because her future depended on Derek's goodwill, *or so she had thought*. But she was beginning to see things in a very different light.

Miguel was not in the least put out. 'Why so angry?' He smiled. 'I only said what we both know to be true.'

The superciliousness Cass saw in his smile snapped her control. 'You know *nothing* about me,' she stormed. 'Like so many of your kind you are arrogant, presumptuous, and extremely rude!'

She froze, her hand flying to her mouth, horrified at her impetuosity.

Miguel Ibarra stiffened, towering over her. One wing-like brow lifted and his bitter-chocolate eyes glittered coldly as they studied her. 'And what do you know of me that qualifies you to make such a damning statement?' he asked with dangerous softness.

An abject apology was already trembling on the tip of Cass's tongue, but somehow she could not utter it. With astonishing clarity she recognised for the first time that she had spent too much time in the past eighteen months apologising for situations which were not of her making. Enough was enough. She had come to Mexico to get away from Derek, but he had followed her. Well, that was *his* decision, she was not responsible for it or for him. Between them Derek and Miguel had more or less forced her into staying at the *hacienda*. She had been given no alternative without causing a scene and appearing rude and ungrateful.

She met his gaze with a mixture of uncertainty and bravado. 'I know only what I see.' Her voice was husky, her throat dry. 'You quite clearly had some preconceived ideas about me. That's *your* problem. I do not have to prove or disprove anything. Nor am I on trial, so I am not obliged to answer your questions. If my refusal offends you, I'm afraid that's just too bad.' She drew in a deep breath. 'And I stand by what I said. You handle that stallion with a gentleness and respect that encourages trust. What a pity you never learned to do the same with people. Now, if you'll excuse me,' she started away towards the stable block.

'Miss Elliott!' His deep voice halted her in mid-stride. She paused, mentally bracing herself, then turned.

'Señor Ibarra?'

His face was inscrutable, but the corners of his chiselled mouth flickered, a movement so fleeting Cass could not be sure whether it signified anger or amusement.

'At ten o'clock I shall be driving into the city. I am expecting a new consignment of stones for cutting. If you would care to accompany me, I am sure you will find it most interesting.'

His gaze held hers. Cass was buffeted by conflicting emotions. She knew instinctively that he was mocking her, yet there was a new light in his dark eyes. She had the strange feeling that he was seeing her for the first time.

Obviously he did not intend to apologise. But despite the undertone, his invitation had been politely phrased, and as part of the purpose of her visit to Mexico was to see gemstones in their natural state and then in the various stages of cutting, to turn it down because of the personal animosity between them would be childish and self-defeating.

'Thank you, Señor Ibarra.' She was equally polite. 'I should be delighted.'

He nodded and led the stallion into the yard and out of sight.

Cass was startled to find herself smiling as she pushed open the front door and ran lightly upstairs to her room.

She had changed her trousers and boots for a tan pleated skirt and elegant court shoes and was putting the finishing touches to a light make-up when there was a tap on the door.

'*Adelante!*' she called, using one of the few Spanish expressions she had learned, expecting Consuelo or one of the maids. But it was Derek who entered.

Closing the door behind him, he leaned against it, smart in a cream shirt and striped tie beneath a dark brown light-weight suit. His hair was neatly brushed and his shoes had a mirror shine. He appeared every inch the smart young executive. Then he looked up and Cass lowered her eyes quickly, smoothing a non-existent crease from her skirt, hiding her shock at the vivid evidence of his hangover. His eyes were bloodshot, his complexion pale and puffy and the bags under his eyes added ten years to his thirty.

'Cass, I don't know what to say.' He shrugged helplessly and thrust his hands into his trouser pockets.

She turned to the mirror, replacing lipstick and comb in her handbag. 'You could try "sorry",' she suggested mildly.

He pushed himself away from the door with his elbows. 'That's what I mean. How can I apologise enough? My behaviour was appalling. Honestly, I'm thoroughly ashamed of myself.' He hung his head and she recognised her cue to forgive and forget. But she had seen that hang-dog look all too often in the past year, and for the same reason.

He glanced up, and she saw a brief surprise cross his features at her continued silence. 'Cass, let me make it up to you.' He came forward and as she turned back to the mirror, rested his hands on her shoulders, rubbing the nape of her neck with his thumbs.

'There's nothing to make up.' She said calmly and, slipping from his grasp, picked up her trousers from the bed and hung them in the wardrobe.

'You still don't understand, do you?' His voice roughened and he grabbed her shoulder, pulling her round to face him. 'Or you *won't*. Cass, you do things to me. I really care about you and all I get is the "keep-off" treatment. Hell, is it any wonder I need the odd drink?'

'That's enough, Derek.' She did not raise her voice, nor did she struggle. She simply stared at him. Yesterday she would have felt guilty, blaming herself for what he was going through. But today she saw it differently. 'You drink because you want to. Your feelings for me, whatever they might be, are just an excuse.'

His chin dropped. He was plainly taken aback. 'Cass——? What—you've never——'

'No, and maybe I should have, a long time ago,' she said gently. She had no desire to hurt him. She looked pointedly at his hand gripping her shoulder and as he released it, she picked up her jacket, 'I think it's time we went down.'

Derek caught her up on the stairs. 'What's the matter with you?' he hissed urgently.

She glanced round in surprise. 'Nothing. Why?'

He was frowning and his chin jutted forward like a stubborn child's. 'You're behaving very oddly. You weren't like this yesterday.'

'Yesterday was a very difficult day for both of us.' She shrugged lightly. 'I certainly don't feel odd. I feel fine, and I'm looking forward to my holiday.'

At the mention of holiday, Derek looked even more dubious. 'I suppose I shall have my work cut out trying to get round Ibarra. No doubt he'll expect me to grovel,' he muttered gloomily.

'A brief apology will probably take care of it,' Cass said. 'But it would be an idea to cut down on the alcohol.' She ignored his defensive glare and went on, 'Apparently it has a much greater effect at this altitude.'

'Another old wives' tale?' Derek scoffed.

'If you consider Miguel Ibarra an old wife,' she shrugged, refusing to be drawn.

They crossed the cool tiled floor of the hall. The

dining-room door stood open and Cass led the way in.
An enormous circular table, on which stood a ceramic
bowl filled with red, yellow and orange marigolds, was
set for three. Silver cutlery, woven rush table mats and
snowy napkins were reflected in the polished wood. On a
massive sideboard a heated tray held several covered
silver dishes. The smell of fresh coffee made Cass's
mouth water.

'You've been talking about me,' Derek accused in a
fierce whisper. 'When did you see him? Did you come
down to dinner last night? What did he say?'

'Please do help yourselves.' Miguel's deep voice saved
Cass from having to answer and she swung round.

He had showered and changed into a pearl-grey suit.
The perfection of its cut and fit made her acutely aware
of his height, his lean athleticism and his long,
powerfully muscled legs. Against the crisp, white shirt
and crimson tie with its small designer motif in the
centre, his skin glowed bronze, and raven-black hair,
still damp, sprang thick and wavy from his broad
forehead to curl against his collar.

Cass's heart gave a sudden extra beat and she turned
away to walk quickly, blindly, towards the sideboard,
feeling as though she had stepped into quicksand. She
heard the scrape of a chair.

'Good morning, Miss Elliott, I trust you slept well?'
Miguel said from somewhere above her left ear as he
reached past to lift the cover from one of the dishes.

'Very well, thank you.' She kept her eyes on the
dishes, raising another cover to reveal lightly fried eggs
swimming in a steaming red sauce. She took a deep
breath. 'In fact I must apologise for missing dinner. I—I
was more tired than I realised.'

'It is of no consequence,' he said dismissively. 'Those
are *huevos rancheros*.' He pointed to the eggs. 'The sauce
is made from tomatoes with spices and a touch of chilli

pepper. It is quite delicious and will not take the roof off your mouth. This we eat with tortillas. You will find them under the cloth.' He indicated a large, shallow, circular basket. 'Perhaps you prefer re-fried beans,' he lifted another cover, 'or tacos, tortillas spread with shredded meat or cheese flavoured with chilli, folded and fried until they are crisp.' He looked over his shoulder at Derek, who, seated at the table, was rubbing his temples with his fingertips. 'Mr Prentice, may I get you something?'

Derek suppressed a shudder. 'No thanks, I'm not hungry. I'll just have coffee.'

'As you like.' Miguel's features tightened imperceptibly as he watched Derek pour himself a cup of strong black coffee with an unsteady hand.

Meanwhile Cass had helped herself to an egg, two spoonfuls of sauce and two tortillas. As she turned to the table, Miguel was there before her, holding her chair. She sat, but before she could reach for her napkin he picked it up and flicked it open, laying it across her lap in the tradition of an attentive *maître d'*.

Cass's cheeks grew warm. She knew he was paying her back for calling him rude and arrogant, but she wasn't sure how to react.

Just for an instant she wished she could think of something really withering to say, something that would put him firmly in his place. Then felt ashamed of herself. After all he *was* trying to make amends and even if they both knew his tongue was very firmly in his cheek, at least he had taken her criticism to heart.

'Thank you,' she said coolly, keeping her eyes firmly on her plate.

'*De nada*.' Then he murmured for her ears only, 'Now eat, the day holds much for you.' Leaving her speechless, he went to the sideboard and filled his own plate.

'Right.' Derek rubbed his hands together with forced joviality. 'What's the plan for today, then?' He leaned towards Miguel, a spasm of nausea contorting his face as his gaze slid hurriedly past his host's full plate. 'You and I must get down to cases, and talk some business, eh, Miguel?'

Cass's fork clattered against her plate as she inwardly cringed at Derek's artificial bonhomie. His hangover was playing havoc with his judgment. Surely he could see that Miguel Ibarra was not the type of man one slapped on the back and had a few drinks with before shoving a contract under his nose? Had Derek done no research at all into Latin-American business methods?

Once again Cass thought of Matthew Prentice. He had always lived by the code that a man's word was his bond, and a handshake as binding as a written agreement.

She had been an unwilling witness to the arguments between Matthew and his son. Derek insisted that his father's beliefs were not only outdated but uneconomic. Profit was the name of today's game. You bought low and sold high. You stitched up your suppliers with contracts making it difficult if not impossible for them to sell to anyone else. You inserted penalty clauses for late deliveries, and passed on all increased charges to the customer.

'You call that business?' Matthew had raged. 'It's robbery, it's ... it's immoral!'

'You have to move with the times, Dad.' Derek had been impatient. 'Competition is that much stiffer now. There isn't room for everyone. If you don't get in there and grab your share, you go under, and what price a gentleman's agreement then? If the business goes bust, morals won't pay the bills.'

The argument had raged back and forth, and Cass, though her heart sided with Matthew and the old ways, could see Derek's point. Maybe father and son represented extremes. Was it not possible there was a more moderate course?

But Derek was visibly fretting under the restraint and though Matthew still retained control, his retirement was drawing nearer, and with it the day when Derek would take over.

More and more lately, Cass had wondered if she would be able to adjust to the sweeping changes Derek planned when he became head of the company.

'Today I will be busy. I am showing Miss Elliott the cutting-rooms,' Miguel replied in a rebuff so calculated that Cass went hot then cold.

But Derek, if he was aware of the snub, chose to ignore it. 'Fine, fine,' he nodded. 'I'll come along too. I want to see the stones myself, take a look at your set-up, all that sort of thing.'

'As you wish.' Miguel's lack of interest was plain.

'Right, then.' Derek stood up. 'Ready when you are. Er, Cass, have you got a couple of aspirin to spare? I guess I'm still a bit jet-lagged.' His attempted smile was more of a grimace and Cass felt a twinge of pity.

'Yes, of course. I'll get them for you.'

He waved her back to her seat as she began to move. 'No need. I can manage. Top drawer as usual?' The artlessness of Derek's question was belied by the glitter in his eyes as they slid towards Miguel.

Cass was stunned. Derek was implying intimate knowledge of her habits, and her bedroom! Miguel Ibarra wasn't to know he had simply made a random guess, a wrong one at that. And nothing she said would erase that first impression. In fact the stronger her protest, the less she would be believed.

But before she could utter a word, Miguel looked up. 'No,' he said evenly, 'the bottle is on the bedside cabinet beside the lamp.'

CHAPTER THREE

THERE was a moment's utter silence. Cass became aware of her own heartbeat growing louder and louder as her horrified gaze flew from Miguel to Derek and back again. She started to get up but Miguel forestalled her.

'Please stay where you are, Miss Elliott, and allow me to pour you more coffee.' His voice was silk over steel. 'You must tell me exactly what you wish to see in our workshops. As it may not be possible for me to remain with you all day——'

Cass found her voice, 'I did not expect it, *señor*,' she responded icily.

He went on as though she had not spoken, '—my assistant will be at your disposal.' He turned his head to fix Derek with a cool stare. 'Was there something else, Mr Prentice?'

Derek flushed brick-red, his face ugly with suppressed fury. His mouth worked, but no words came out. Then he whirled round and stormed out.

Cass was almost as angry. 'How dare you!' she spluttered. 'You had no right to—to——'

'To what?' Miguel asked calmly. 'To allow you to sleep when that was what you so clearly needed? To protect you from the night chill? The dark hours are cold up here. Would you wish your stay spoiled by illness?'

'No, of course not, but——'

'Your *friend*,' he interrupted, investing the term with a wealth of scorn, 'was using you to score a cheap point. I will not have my guests abused in such a manner.'

Cass jumped to her feet. 'How very thoughtful of

you!' she blazed. 'And of course you had no intention of doing the same!'

One dark brow lifted. 'I do not understand.'

'I bet you don't.' Cass flung the words at him. 'Naturally it never occurred to you that Derek would wonder how *you* knew where the aspirins were, how you could *possibly* know unless you had been in my bedroom.'

Miguel's eyes narrowed. 'You are not betrothed to him.' It was a statement.

'No, but——'

'And you do not intend to be.'

'No——'

'Then whom you invite to your room is not his concern.'

'But I *didn't* invite you,' Cass cried.

'You know that and I know that,' Miguel said imperturbably, 'so where is the problem?' He leaned forward, resting one arm on the table, his dark eyes intent. 'If I had permitted you to leave this room and go upstairs, do you think *he* would have shared that view?'

Cass stared at him. What he said was true. Derek would have subjected her to a barrage of questions, demanding answers as though by right.

But she owed *no one* any explanations. She was her own person, free to do as she liked. The realisation filled her with a strange mixture of exultation and dismay, for it made her future even more uncertain. Having discovered this new self, she could not deny it, but Derek would not easily accept the sudden change. The fact that he was involved in her career made it doubly difficult.

'So,' Miguel stood up, breaking into her thoughts, 'you are ready?' His gaze held hers across the litter of the meal and she read challenge in it.

She lifted her chin. 'Ready.' Her throat was dry but

her heels clicked briskly on the tiles as she picked up her bag and walked out into the hall.

Derek met them at the bottom of the stairs, but Miguel did not allow Cass's pace to falter.

Acutely aware of his hand resting lightly on the small of her back and anxious to escape the unsettling touch, Cass climbed into the pale blue and ivory Range Rover, not realising until he closed the door and was half-way round the bonnet that he had seated her in the front next to himself.

Derek got in the back, slamming the door with unnecessary force as Miguel fastened his seat-belt and started the engine. By then it was too late to change anything.

Miguel guided the vehicle down the drive and on to the rough road. Derek's smouldering resentment added to an atmosphere already tense. But Miguel seemed oblivious as he replied to Cass's rather desperate observation that the colours of the car matched those of the helicopter.

'It's a form of advertising of course, though, naturally, we do not use our name.'

'Oh, naturally,' Derek muttered sarcastically.

'Why not?' Cass asked, pretending not to hear.

'It is not necessary. My father chose the combination of colours and the design. It is unique, our trademark if you like.'

Cass was intrigued. 'Could you have chosen any colours you wanted?'

He nodded. 'Provided we did not infringe anyone else's design.'

'Why ivory and blue?' Derek demanded from the back. 'Pastel shades are hardly part of the macho image, I'd have thought.'

Miguel's eyes flickered to the rear-view mirror and a muscle jumped in his jaw but his voice remained even.

'Here in Mexico the machine is operating in what are termed "hot and high" conditions. Pale colours have greater reflective powers. There is the other point that the arrangement of colours, ivory at the top over the engine casing and front of the cabin, and blue running from the door to the tail, increases the illusion of length and minimises the helicopter's tadpole appearance.' He caught Cass's darted glance. 'You seem surprised,' he said drily.

Cass hesitated, but only for a moment. She and the tall man beside her had been far too bruisingly honest with one another for circumspection to carry any weight now. 'I wouldn't have thought appearances bothered you,' she said recklessly.

'They don't,' he agreed, 'not for their own sake. But certain shapes are more aesthetically pleasing than others.' He turned his head, impaling her with a penetrating glance. Her breath caught in her throat as her heart kicked.

'I am as susceptible to beauty as any man and more fortunate than most,' he turned once more to the windscreen, 'for my life is full of it: my horses, the gemstones I handle every day, even these hills.'

'And women?' Derek's tone was half-snigger, half-sneer, and Cass felt both ashamed and irritated at his continued sniping.

But though her intuition, so startlingly acute where Miguel was concerned, told her he was becoming progressively more irritated by Derek's manner, not by so much as the flicker of an eyelid did he betray it.

'Indeed, there are many beautiful women in my country,' he said impassively.

'You were talking about *your* life,' Derek argued. 'How many beautiful women do *you* know ... *personally*?'

It suddenly dawned on Cass that despite his apparent

banter, Derek was not only trying to embarrass Miguel, he was also having a go at *her*, warning her off, making it plain, without actually saying so, that she was wasting her time if she harboured any fanciful thoughts about attracting the handsome Mexican.

Compressing her lips, she seethed in silence and stared out of the side window, her long hair curving forward, masking her face from them both as she battled to contain a mixture of emotions that were deeply disturbing. She could say nothing without bringing Derek's insinuations to Miguel's attention, and that was the *last* thing she wanted to do.

'I have never felt it necessary to count,' Miguel replied coolly and, making it clear the subject was closed, he touched Cass's hand lightly to attract her attention before pointing to the hillside. 'As you see, our crops are somewhat different from those in your country.'

Her cheeks pink, conscious of the lingering imprint of his fingers, Cass kept her gaze focused outside. 'What *is* that? There were fields of it near the airstrip.'

'Agave, a species of maguey. They look like cacti, but in fact are not.'

'What are they for?' Cass forced her attention outside to her surroundings. 'I mean, do you eat them?'

'These are not grown as a food plant,' he explained, 'though other species, as well as providing paper and thread, also supply vinegar, molasses and candy. Did you notice that the root looks rather like a large hand-grenade?'

Cass turned to him. 'Is that significant?'

He nodded. 'You have heard of tequila, the national drink of Mexico?'

'It was once described to me as liquid fire.'

He grimaced. 'That seems reasonably accurate. Tequila is distilled from agave roots, and if you are not used to it,' he grinned at her, 'it will blow your head off.'

Cass felt herself begin to relax. 'Do you grow much?'

'Several thousand acres.'

As she gasped, Miguel shrugged. 'Up here the ground is not fit for anything else.'

'Is that why you have the helicopter?' she ventured. 'To get around the estate?'

'Partly. Though we have foremen with walkie-talkies covering different areas in trucks or on horseback. The helicopter is used more for trips between the *hacienda* and our mines, and of course, San Miguel.'

Cass looked blank, then asked uncertainly, 'What is San Miguel?'

'A town about forty miles from here.' He was silent for a moment. 'In his letter I believe my father suggested that you should attend a fiesta?'

'Yes.' Cass couldn't entirely banish the disappointment from her voice. She had read about the loud and colourful celebrations where singing and dancing blended with devotions to the saint in whose honour the fiesta was being held. But no books could fully convey the unique blend of carnival and religious pilgrimage which comprised the event. 'It's such a pity——' She broke off, suddenly ashamed. 'I'm sorry, that was thoughtless of me. Naturally, with your father so ill, you have far more on your mind than fiestas.'

He gave her a thoughtful look, but remained silent.

They drove through the outskirts of the city, past shanties where Indians and Mestizo peasants lived side by side. Ragged children played barefoot in the dust. Women sat in their doorways, sewing and gossiping in the sunshine. An old man in broken sandals shuffled along with two white chickens tucked under his arms and was passed by a boy whose torn shorts reached almost to his knees, carrying an enormous basket of fresh flowers.

'God,' Derek muttered in disgust, 'how can they live like that?'

'They do the best they can with what they have,' Miguel replied. His voice had an edge to it.

'It's utter squalor,' Derek shuddered. 'What are they doing here anyway? Where have they come from?' He swivelled round to watch through the back window two Indian girls in red-sashed cotton skirts and embroidered blouses squatting beside a small fire over which stood an iron griddle. Their hair fell over their shoulders in a single braid tied with ribbon as they patted lumps of dough between floury hands into flat round cakes, laying them on a chipped plate next to the fire.

'If you mean those girls,' Miguel said, 'they have not come from anywhere. They are Otomi Indians. This town was founded by their ancestors. It became part of the Aztec empire in the fifteenth century, and was captured by the Spanish in 1531. Those girls have more right to be here than you or I.'

'Has your family lived here long?' Cass blurted, anxious to deter Derek from making any more scathing remarks. It was obvious he and Miguel did not like one another, but couldn't he see that if he stretched Miguel's tolerance too far he might as well wave goodbye to any hopes of a business agreement? She realised she was tense again, wound up tight as a watch-spring. It was reaction born of habit. She was trying to keep the peace, using herself as a buffer between the two men. *Why* was she doing it? No one had asked her to. As she recognised this truth, another was demanding to be faced—her growing curiosity about Miguel Ibarra. He was everything she had accused him of, and more. Yet their short acquaintanceship had affected her more deeply than she cared to admit.

It wasn't simply his physical impact, though that was profound. He rode superbly, drove with an economy of style that mocked Derek's 'macho' image, and piloted his own helicopter. There was nothing ostentatious about his undeniable wealth and he was plainly more than capable of handling the Ibarra business empire in his father's absence. He was the ultimate modern man.

And yet—Cass had a vivid recollection of an illustration of Montezuma, the Aztec emperor. His gold-threaded robes, gem-encrusted sandals, and cloak of shimmering green feathers had impressed her less than his features. He had demanded the sacrifice of thousands of human hearts, believing that without this offering the sun would refuse to rise. His empire had been one of the most well organised and fabulously wealthy the world had ever known. It was also the cruellest.

Cass darted a glance at Miguel, seeing in his profile echoes of the past. Gooseflesh erupted on her arms and despite the sun's warmth and the comfort of the car, she shivered. She tried to convince herself that all she saw was the same strength of purpose, and failed. It was more than that, much more.

'How long? Over four hundred years,' he said casually. 'One of my ancestors came from Spain with the conquistadors. The woman he married was already here.'

Cass felt a strange sinking sensation in the pit of her stomach. They passed an ornate church topped with domes and towers. A tree-lined plaza was thronged with people representing every level of society. Indian women squatted beside stone troughs which spilled brilliant flowers on to the grey paving, selling hand-made artefacts and embroidered blouses. Sober-suited businessmen strode briskly, briefcases swinging, towards offices. Mestizo youths with small boxes of tools lounged against railings holding up cards displaying their willingness to undertake electrical, plumbing or car repairs immediately.

She saw it all and took none of it in. Miguel guided the car down a wide thoroughfare lined with shops and offices. 'Come, Miss Elliott,' his deep voice was heavy with irony, 'don't pretend you didn't know.'

Cass's lips were dry and she moistened them with the tip of her tongue. It *couldn't* be. But she had to ask, *she had to know*. 'The woman, was she——' Cass fumbled for the right words '—of high or low birth?'

Miguel drew the car to a stop outside an imposing colonial building with outward-curving wrought-iron bars screening the long windows on the ground floor. He turned to look at her, his eyes very dark. 'She was not Otomi,' he said softly. 'She was Aztec. As for her rank, does it matter?' His tone was careless but there was an intentness in his gaze that demanded total honesty.

'No,' she said simply.

'Look, what's all this about?' Derek leaned forward, resting his arms on the back of Cass's seat. 'Have I missed something important?'

'To you, no.' Miguel tossed the words over his shoulder, his eyes never leaving Cass's. 'You are very observant.' It sounded almost like an accusation.

'I am an artist,' she shrugged helplessly.

The combination of a hangover, no breakfast and antipathy towards his host had frayed Derek's nerves to breaking point. 'For God's sake, stop talking in riddles. Are you two having some sort of joke at my expense?'

'You really are too suspicious,' Miguel chided and Cass uncurled fingers that had clenched in anticipation of an explosion. 'One of the many differences between you and Miss Elliott is that you see only what you choose to see, while she——' Beneath his probing gaze she grew warm and her lashes fluttered down before he could read in her eyes the first stirrings of a momentous and terrifying realisation, something for which she was totally unprepared.

'She sees what is there,' he finished and, opening the door, slid out of the car with fluid ease and was round to help Cass out before she had managed to unfasten her seat-belt.

His hand beneath her elbow was a simple courtesy, yet the touch and his very nearness reinforced the subtle spell he had, whether by accident or design, been weaving around her since their row in the paddock that morning.

The massive outer door stood open and Miguel led her through double doors of toughened glass that whispered apart as they approached.

The air-conditioned reception area was floored with marble. In one corner jasmine climbed a fine trellis, perfuming the air. A comfortable settee and several chairs were grouped around a low table over which were scattered glossy magazines printed in Spanish, English and Portuguese.

Behind the semi-circular reception desk, on which stood a sophisticated telecommunications system, an electric typewriter, trays of letters and forms and an open notebook, sat an attractive woman. Cass guessed her to be about thirty.

Dressed in a classic suit of oyster-grey with a lilac silk ruffled blouse, her dark hair was swept up into a smooth pleat revealing earrings of polished amethyst surrounded by tiny seed pearls. Her voice as she greeted Miguel in Spanish was low-pitched and pleasant.

'Good morning, Luisa,' Miguel responded in English, and Cass was touched by the gesture, evidence of the faultless manners which were instinctive to him when he wasn't in one of his arrogant moods.

Miguel paused to take the sheaf of messages she handed to him, but made no effort to introduce the woman. From that Cass deduced that, despite their ease of manner, the woman was an employee and not a

personal friend. Cass wondered at her own sense of
relief, quickly wrenching her thoughts away from the
dangerous path they were taking.

'I must say, I like the window-dressing,' Derek
muttered in Cass's ear, and she glanced to see him eyeing
Luisa through narrowed lids.

'Is Benito in?' Miguel asked, flicking through the
slips.

'Yes, *señor*, and no, there is no news yet. I tell him he
should relax or he will be exhausted when the time
comes.' Her English, though heavily accented, was
fluent, and her eyes as she smiled at her employer were
serene.

Miguel returned her smile, enjoying the shared joke.
'How much longer can we survive? I thought it was
supposed to get easier.'

'For Benito, or for his wife?' Luisa's elegant brows
arched in gentle irony.

Miguel laughed deep in his throat and, shaking his
head, guided Cass towards one of the doors leading from
the reception area. Unlike the others, which were of
plain wood, this one had panels of toughened glass and
appeared to be of double thickness.

Luisa pressed a button on an unmarked console beside
the switchboard and with a muffled *thunk* the door
unlocked. Miguel pushed it open and held it for Cass and
Derek to walk through.

'That's quite some security system,' Derek remarked
with a trace of envy.

'It has proved well worth the investment,' Miguel
replied, leading them down a well lit passage with doors
on either side. 'We still have an occasional attempted
break-in, but word must have got around, for they are
few and far between. Now, I will show you first some of
our finished stones.' He stopped outside what looked like
a plain wooden door, but set in the wall at one side was a

row of small buttons with numbers on. Though Miguel stood between them and the buttons, he must have pressed in a sequence of numbers because after another click, the door slid sideways into a recess in the wall.

As they entered the small room, a guard, sitting reading a newspaper, jumped to his feet. Behind him was a huge safe with a combination lock.

'If you please, Pedro,' Miguel gestured.

'*Sí, señor.*' The man, a beefy six-footer in a uniform of khaki shirt and trousers, came towards them and Cass's eyes widened as she realised he was wearing a gun.

'Do you object to your bag being searched?' Miguel asked her.

'N-no.' She opened her bag and passed it to the guard who quickly checked the contents, giving it back to her with a polite nod. Then turning, he ran his hands with swift expertise over Derek's jacket and trousers, right to his ankles.

'Going a bit far, isn't it?' Derek sniffed. 'Do all your guests get this treatment?'

'All those who come in here,' Miguel replied calmly. 'At any one time we have hundreds of thousands of dollars' worth of cut gems in this safe. They are my responsibility. The people who send them here for cutting and polishing trust me to protect their property. I am merely honouring that trust.'

'Well, OK,' Derek grudged, 'but still,' he looked at the guard, 'I mean, you must be insured.'

Miguel stared at him. 'Of course. But what has that to do with it?'

Again Cass was vividly aware of the difference between the two men. She had frequently heard Derek referred to in tones of admiration as 'a damn good businessman'. Yet learning the details of a deal he had set up or pulled off, she had often been left with a deep sense of unease. Activities which appeared commonplace if not actually compulsory were all too often questionable to say the least.

The guard stood in front of Cass and Derek while Miguel spun the combination then turned the wheel on the front of the safe. The door swung silently open and the guard retired to his chair alongside the door.

'Please, sit down.' Miguel gestured towards a metal table covered with pale grey baize and screwed to the floor with heavy bolts. Above the table two spotlights, their bulbs covered in fine steel mesh, were attached to the wall.

Looking for chairs, Cass did not at first notice the small, padded backless seats, each fixed on a hinge to the legs of the table.

'Good God!' Derek shook his head in reluctant amazement. 'You thought of everything, didn't you? There's nothing in this room that can be moved, lifted or broken. Not one potential weapon.'

Turning from the safe with a velvet-covered tray in his hands, Miguel simply inclined his head in acknowledgement. He switched on the spotlights, directing their beam on to the tray as he set it down before Cass. Then he sat beside her. His height and breadth of shoulder and the fixed seats brought him unnervingly close, but there was no way of widening the distance between them.

'These are all white opals,' Miguel explained.

The smoothly rounded gems, pearly against the black velvet, were shot through with brilliant streaks of scarlet, ice-blue and vivid emerald.

'Where are they from?' Derek asked. 'Is this the sort of stuff your mines produce?'

'These are from La Esperanza,' Miguel replied, 'near San Juan del Rio. It was Mexico's first important opal mine and has been worked since its discovery in 1835. They are not ours. However, our own mines produce gems of equal if not superior quality.'

'What actually causes the incandescence?' Cass bent her head to study the stones more closely. Of varying sizes and shapes, the only things they had in common were their rounded finish and milky background. In every stone the play of shimmering colour was different.

'Diffracted light, basically,' Miguel replied. 'Opal is a silica mineral, a sub-microcrystalline variety of cristabo-lite. Light enters through cracks in the stone and is reflected off a three-dimensional lattice of minute round particles producing spectral colours.'

'Of course,' Derek's sarcastic mutter was ignored, though Cass flinched inwardly.

She gazed at the gems. 'For me, they're fragments of a rainbow.' She glanced up at Miguel. 'Isn't it odd how many superstitions have been attached to opals.'

He nodded. 'The Romans considered them noble gems and ranked them second only to emeralds. In the Middle Ages they were considered a lucky stone. Now some people refuse to wear them because they're *unlucky.*'

'I think they've gained that reputation because in certain climatic conditions they shrink or crack,' Cass said.

'That is possible,' Miguel allowed. 'Even so, no woman who favours a strong perfume will ever wear opals successfully.'

Cass twisted round to look at him. 'Is that another superstition?'

He shook his head. 'Chemistry.' His dark eyes glittered.

Cass's gaze slid shyly back to the stones. 'H-how are they formed? Where do they come from?'

'The action of hot springs deposits the mineral in cavities in volcanic rocks. Opal itself contains five to ten per cent water and can absorb a lot more.' His voice, deep and soft, feathered down her spine and she felt herself growing warm, despite the air-conditioning.

She stared at the tray, the stones dancing before her eyes, aware of her deepening colour, aware of his heavy-lidded scrutiny. 'I——' She cleared her throat and began again. 'I always protect the opals I use with a film of oil to prevent them drying out. I find it helps preserve their colour as well.' Even to herself her voice sounded strained. Why did he stare so? Why did it disconcert her? Why couldn't she ignore it, or shrug it aside, or pretend it wasn't happening? She was twenty-five years old and, though no worldly-wise sophisticate, neither was she a gauche adolescent. Yet there was something about him that fascinated even as it perturbed her. A complex mixture of traditional and contemporary, of imperiousness and tolerance, this man was unlike any she had ever met.

He linked his fingers, resting his forearms on the table.

'As you are already aware, our mines produce many cat's-eye and harlequin opals. But a few weeks ago a small pocket of rare water opal known as contra luz was discovered.'

'I've heard of that particular gem,' Cass put in, fighting an awareness that their conversation was taking place on two separate levels. His words said one thing, but his eyes and the tone of his voice said another. But she couldn't afford to listen. She did not want to hear. She could not deny the attraction she felt for him, nor could she any longer tell herself he was totally uninterested in her, the opposite was becoming all too plain. But she was only just beginning to discover herself. She had not broken free from Derek's domination only to dance to another man's tune, no matter how captivating the melody.

'But I've never used contra luz,' she babbled on. 'As the iridescence can only be seen by transmitted light, the stones are not immediately impressive, so I don't think they would be suitable for my jewellery.' She turned aside from the table, swivelling round on the padded seat, her knees brushing his thigh. It was impossible to remain sitting so close to him in the small room with Derek glaring suspiciously at Miguel then herself. 'We are imposing on your kindness, *señor*. You said yourself you had many other things to do.' She raised her eyes briefly.

His features were a mask of impassivity but his voice was clipped and harsh. 'Forgive me. I had no wish to bore you.'

From the corner of her vision she saw Derek roll his eyes in relief. But she could not allow Miguel to think she was bored. Nothing was further from the truth. Nervous, certainly; tense, yes; but bored? Never. 'Oh no,' she exclaimed, laying an impulsive hand on his arm. 'You're not, truly. It wasn't—I mean, I didn't——' She took her hand away quickly, aware of the heat radiating from her flushed face. 'Please, I'd love to see some more.'

'Well, I have to say this side of the business really isn't my scene.' Derek stood up. 'I'm a figures man myself. Show me a set of accounts and I'll tell you all there is to know about that business. I've never believed in keeping a dog and barking myself. I rely on my staff experts for appraisal of quality.'

'Derek!' Cass blurted, shocked as much by his blatant disrespect as his attempt to present himself as head of the company. 'Your father buys all our stones.'

'Sure,' he agreed innocently, lifting one shoulder in a careless shrug, 'didn't I just say that?' He turned to Miguel. 'Mind if I take a look at the safe? Can't say I've seen one like that before.'

Miguel rose to his feet and picked up the tray. 'Not at all.' His voice was expressionless. Derek followed him as he replaced the tray and took out another, covered this time in pale cream velvet. He straightened up. 'But please, do not touch anything.'

Derek's mouth tightened in indignation and resentment, but he made no comment. Turning his back on them both he pushed his hands into his trouser pockets and leaned forward to examine the locking mechanism more closely.

Miguel placed the tray in front of Cass but instead of resuming his seat, he leaned over her, resting one hand on the table while with the other he peeled back the square of velvet covering the stones.

'Ohhh!' Cass's soft intake of breath prompted a smile that softened Miguel's slightly cruel mouth. She glanced up at him then turned back wide-eyed to the gems. 'They're ... fabulous!'

'*Girasol del fuego*, the fire opal,' he said quietly, and lifting a lock of her hair let it spill over his fingers. 'It was created for you, Cassandra.'

Cass sat very still, hardly breathing, burningly aware of the intimacy both of his gesture and his use of her name. She stared at the facet-cut stones that ranged in colour from translucent orange to fiery red, every nerve taut, vibrating with mingled uncertainty and anticipation.

Releasing the silky tress, Miguel lifted a corner of the tray. In the middle, surrounded by smaller gems, one oblong stone the size of Cass's little fingernail flashed incandescent flame from a rich crimson centre.

'What do you think of it?' he asked softly.

Cass shook her head, unable to take her eyes off the stone. 'It's exquisite,' she whispered. 'Do you get many like that?'

'No,' he admitted. 'It's the finest I have ever seen.'

'It would make a beautiful ring.' She was not aware of the wistfulness in her tone.

'You would not use it as the centre-stone in a necklace?' He moved the tray again and the opal was a living flame.

'Oh, no.' Cass was definite. 'A stone like that is unique, matchless. To mount it with others would detract from both it and them. I——' she hesitated, 'I suppose it's very expensive?' She did not want it for its value. She wanted it for its sheer, unsurpassed beauty. Oh, how she wanted it!

Miguel gently replaced the velvet over the gems. 'It would be, if it were for sale.'

Disappointment washed over her in a cold wave, but she couldn't give up. 'Does it belong to one of your clients? Do you think they might be persuaded to sell? I would pay full market price.'

'I'm afraid not,' he said firmly. 'As a matter of fact the stone is to be made into a ring. I know the owner well. No amount of money would persuade him to part with it.'

Cass made a brave attempt to smile. 'Oh well, he has excellent taste. It will make a beautiful ring. I hope he has the sense to make it a solitaire, or better yet, surround it with diamonds to bring out the fire at its heart.'

Miguel opened his mouth to reply but his words were drowned by an ear-splitting cacophony of electric alarm bells.

CHAPTER FOUR

CASS and Miguel whirled round. The guard sprang to his feet and lunged forward, one hand flying to his gun.

'Pedro!' Miguel's quick cry froze the man in a semi-crouch.

The colour had drained from Derek's face, leaving it ashen as he cringed away from the guard.

At a nod from Miguel, Pedro straightened up slowly, and reaching for a hidden switch, turned off the alarm. He remained poised for action, balanced on the balls of his feet, staring fixedly at Derek as he waited for instructions.

The silence was deafening. Derek pushed his hands into his pockets and shrugged. He attempted to grin. 'Just testing.'

Cass released the breath she had been holding in a soft rush as Miguel crossed to a wall phone behind the guard's chair and punched in a number.

'Luisa? The alarm was set off accidentally. I repeat, it was an accident. Please notify the rest of the staff at once. I'll inform the police from here.' He cleared the line.

'I say,' Derek interrupted uncomfortably, 'is that really necessary. I mean——'

'This system is on a direct link to Police Headquarters.' Miguel was terse. 'They do not appreciate hoax calls.' He punched in more numbers and spoke in rapid-fire Spanish. Then, after making what Cass deduced from his tone was an apology, he replaced the receiver with slow deliberation.

There was no trace of friendliness on the bronze features now. Derek had backed away from the safe and

54

now stood beside Cass. As Miguel's laser-like gaze surveyed them in turn, it was as though an invisible but impenetrable wall had sprung up, with them on one side and him on the other. His expression was cold, his eyes opaque, revealing no emotion whatsoever.

'Mr Prentice, did you touch any of the stones?'

Cass felt real fear, like slivers of ice, trickle down her spine at the flinty tone. The sight of the armed guard just to one side of Miguel reminded her with stunning force that she was in a foreign country, far from everything familiar. The tall man whose chilling gaze flickered from Derek to herself was once more a total stranger.

'No.' Once he had spoken, Derek seemed to regain his confidence and Cass watched him straighten his back and puff out his chest. 'No,' he repeated, more strongly this time, defying doubt. 'No, of couse not. I must have brushed against something, that's all. Shall I turn out my pockets? Do you want your tame gorilla to search me again?

'No, Mr Prentice,' Miguel replied quietly and held out his hand to Cass. Automatically she picked up the tray of fire opals from the table and passed it to him. It was only afterwards that she realised he had not asked for them, he had not needed to. She had *known* what he wanted. She clasped her arms across her chest, suddenly shaky.

'You are my guest,' Miguel went on. 'Naturally, I accept your word.' Derek would have spoken then, but Miguel's quiet tones over-rode him. 'If you have lied to me, I have lost only a jewel, and, as you pointed out, I am insured. Though in such circumstances no claim would be made. Whereas you,' he paused and though it was Derek he was looking at, Cass flinched at what she saw in his eyes, 'you would have lost something irreplaceable.'

Derek flushed brick-red. 'Now look here,' he blustered, 'I said it was an accident.'

Cass knew in that moment that he was lying. There was not enough righteous indignation, or even quiet conviction, for him to be telling the truth.

'So you did,' Miguel agreed coolly and, turning, slid the tray into the safe. He closed the massive door and tightened the wheel before spinning the combination dial.

'Now you must excuse me. As Miss Elliott so thoughtfully pointed out, I have many other matters to attend to.' With a brief nod to the guard who resumed his seat, Miguel pressed a button on the wall. The door slid back and he stood aside, gesturing for them to precede him.

Cass snatched up her bag from the table and walked quickly out. She felt shunned, bereft. Did Miguel think *she* was somehow involved in what Derek had done? What *had* he done? Why did Miguel suspect it was something more than a stupid, careless accident?

As they reached the security door into the reception area, Miguel leaned past her to press a button on the wall. Cass saw Luisa glance up and reach for the release button on her desk. The lock disengaged and Miguel opened the door and held it for her. As she passed him their eyes met for a brief instant. His expression was unreadable but one wing-like brow lifted fractionally.

She felt heat surge in her own face. Then pride tilted her chin. There was no reason why she should feel guilty. And yet, as Derek pushed past her to slump down on one of the easy chairs, she could not entirely erase the nagging doubts.

'Please sit down, Miss Elliott.' His tone was utterly impersonal and in total contrast to his use of her first name. She lowered her eyes swiftly so that he should not see her unexpected sadness. 'My assistant, Benito Suarez, will be with you both in a moment. He will take you to lunch and afterwards will show you the cutting-rooms.'

Cass turned to Miguel in surprise, but before she could speak Derek chipped in. 'You mean we're not on the next plane out? No pointing fingers? No claims that I'm out to rob you with the help of my moll here?'

'Derek!' For heaven's sake!' Cass bit down hard on embarrassed anger. 'In the circumstances, that is not at all funny.'

Malice glittered in Derek's eyes and thinned his mouth. He leaned back in his chair and, crossing his legs began to swing one foot. 'Your only fault, my love, is that you have no sense of humour.' He spread one hand. 'It was only a joke. Miguel knows that, don't you, Miguel?' He grinned up at the Mexican, whose features remained impassive.

'Perhaps Miss Elliott finds, as I do, that humour is a matter of personal taste. As for the rest,' Miguel's eyes narrowed, 'no one has yet succeeded in taking what is mine.' He gave a bleak smile. 'I do not foresee any change.' He inclined his head in brief farewell and turned away.

Cass watched his tall figure disappear through one of the unmarked doors, then sank back in her chair. Her forehead puckered in a frown as questions clamoured in her brain. She looked up, only to see Derek already watching her, his bottom lip thrust forward in sulky defiance.

'Don't you start on me, Cass,' he warned. 'OK, so I went a bit over the top, but he acts so bloody superior, he gets up my nose.'

It occurred to Cass to retort that Miguel didn't *have* to act, he *was* superior, but there was no point in adding fuel to Derek's already smouldering resentment. She took a deep breath and tried very hard to sound reasonable. 'Do you honestly think you are presenting yourself, and the Prentice company, in the best light carrying on like this?' She saw his mouth tighten, and leaned forward. 'Derek, I'm not having a go at you, I'm just asking you to try and be objective. Why on earth should Miguel Ibarra commit himself to a business deal with someone who appears to be quite deliberately flouting all the basic rules of courtesy?'

He glared at her. 'Is that what you think I'm doing?'

'Well, isn't it?' she shot back.

'Perhaps.' Derek flung one arm over the back of his chair and gazed round the reception area. 'But he'll sign,' he said confidently.

Cass sighed with exasperation. 'How can you be so sure? He must have dozens of other outlets for his gems besides us. In fact, we're very small fry compared with the international companies. And Derek,' she lowered her voice, 'with his wealth he doesn't exactly *need* our custom.'

'No,' Derek agreed. Uncrossing his legs, he rested his forearms on his knees, leaning towards her. 'But he's taken a fancy to you and that puts us right out in front, doesn't it?' His conspiratorial smile was edged with bitterness.

'D-don't be ridiculous!' A wave of heat flooded through Cass and she knew her high colour betrayed very mixed feelings. 'If Miguel Ibarra has shown particular courtesy towards me, it's probably to make up for *your* behaviour. You haven't exactly gone out of your way to win friends and influence people since we arrived,' she whispered fiercely.

'I wouldn't call stroking your hair mere *courtesy*,' Derek jibed, ignoring the rest of her remarks.

Cass's colour deepened. What could she say? It had been an extraordinarily intimate thing to do.

'Anyway,' Derek muttered, 'don't pretend you don't know *why* I've been a bit touchy. You've been playing hard to get, and I know why. It's got to be marriage or nothing for you hasn't it? OK, if that's what it takes, you've got it. We'll tie the knot as soon as we get back. I know it's what Dad's been hoping for.' He spread his fingers. 'I guess I knew you wouldn't settle for less, even though I always swore no woman would ever tie me down. Anyway,' he rubbed his hands together briskly, 'now that's settled, you don't need to lead Ibarra on any more. You were out of your league there in any case. Mind you,' he added hastily as an afterthought, 'you needn't exactly give him the cold shoulder either. The deal wasn't the main reason I came out here, but why spoil a good opportunity? If he thinks you've cooled off, it could cost us a packet.'

Speechless, Cass stared at the man opposite her. A man she had thought she knew. She couldn't believe what she had just heard. 'Do you mean you've been acting like a spoilt child because you thought I wanted a proposal of *marriage* from you?' Even as she said the words she could scarcely credit the ego and self-centredness behind his reasoning.

Derek shifted in his chair. 'Well, it's quite a price you're demanding.' He sounded almost accusatory. 'I mean, we're both free and over twenty-one. You know I want you, I've made that clear enough. I was quite prepared to make it a one-to-one relationship.' He was oblivious of the effect his words were having on her. 'I just didn't see the need for bits of paper. Women seem to have this hang-up about investing a perfectly normal biological urge with all sorts of emotional stuff— ceremony and commitment—which really just confuses the issue. But,' he flashed her what he imagined was a winning smile, 'if that's what it takes to make you mine, you got it, kid.'

A few moments earlier Cass had felt like laughing at the sheer ridiculousness of the situation. But now it wasn't funny any more, and suddenly she was so *mad*, so furiously angry, she felt dizzy. Clenching her teeth together so tightly her jaws ached, she did not dare utter a single word, for if she had, there would have been no stemming the torrent of passionate indignation that seethed within her. But common sense and her natural consideration for other people warned her that the reception area of Miguel Ibarra's business headquarters was not the place to express her feelings. So, almost literally choking on her rage, she stared at the floor, battling for control.

'Look, I can see you're a bit overcome.' She heard Derek's voice as if from a distance. 'I guess I'm rather surprised myself. Never thought anyone would actually get me to take the plunge. We'll talk tonight, after dinner. Tell you what, while we're in town, I'll pick up a bottle of brandy.'

'I wouldn't bother, Derek,' Cass said tersely.

'Well, I'm not going to toast our future in Ibarra's booze. Besides,' his voice dropped, growing slightly hoarse, 'it will help you loosen up a bit, you know, throw off some of those old inhibitions.'

Slowly, her hands white-knuckled with strain, Cass raised her eyes to his, reading in them eagerness and something more, something which made her recoil inwardly.

'Derek,' she began, but got no further, interrrupted by the sound of a door slamming and footsteps hurrying across the floor towards them. Cass looked round quickly.

The man was short and stocky. His curly hair, cropped close to his skull, was already receding despite the youthfulness of his round face. The jacket of his brown suit flapped open to reveal a waistcoat whose buttons strained across a pronounced paunch and his quick, short strides reminded Cass of a pigeon.

He beamed, extending both arms in a wide gesture of welcome. 'Good afternoon, Mees Ell-i-ott,' he pronounced her name with great care, separating the syllables, 'and to you, Meestair Prentice. I am Benito Suarez, the assistant of Don Miguel.'

Cass rose gracefully to her feet, warming to the little man's transparent goodwill as she shook the outstretched hand. 'It is most kind of you to spare us your time, Sěnor Suarez.'

'Ees my pleasure.' He beamed expansively and leaned past Cass. The lack of enthusiasm in Derek's brief greeting went unnoticed. 'I think is best we eat now before restaurant become full. I want very much to hear about England——' behind her Cass heard Derek groan '—and ees possible you have questions about my country or about the works of cutting the beautiful stones which come here from many places. You like that?'

'Well, actually old son, if it's all the same to you——' Derek began but Cass interrupted.

'That sounds marvellous,' she said quickly.

Benito beamed again, happily oblivious of the crackling tension surrounding Cass. 'So, we go and eat.' He bowed her through the glass doors and out on to the crowded street.

The noise had the force of a blow. Cars hooted, engines roared, vendors shouted and rang handbells as people talked and laughed, adding to the din. Overloaded trucks creaked past, belching exhaust fumes into air redolent of flowers, oil, roasting coffee, bad drains and the ever present chilli spice.

Mexicans of every shade, facial conformation and level of society rubbed shoulders on the wide pavement.

'Is no far,' Benito reassured, trotting along beside Cass as they were jostled and bumped. She clutched her bag more tightly, then he touched her arm, guiding her through an old-fashioned wood-panelled door with small, square panes of glass in its upper half, barely twenty yards from the building they had just left.

Red and white check curtains matched the crisp cloths covering the small round tables. Potted plants on a high shelf trailed lush greenery down panelled walls. The varnished floor was spotless and the spicy smell of cooking food made Cass's mouth water.

The only concession to modernity was a brightly lit glass and metal counter behind which different entrées were displayed on a hot tray.

'Is all Mexican dishes,' Benito explained, 'but if you no like, is possible to ask for some other thing. Come, we sit here. Is plenty room.' He had chosen a table by the window.

Cass was surprised and touched when Benito held her chair and passed her a napkin before seating himself. The courtesy appeared to irritate Derek who had already sat down. He scowled but Cass simply ignored him.

'I think I'll have enchiladas, cheese ones,' she announced, passing the menu to Derek.

Benito's eyebrows shot up. 'You know already Mexican food?' He looked delighted.

'Not really, but Miguel—Sēnor Ibarra,' she corrected herself hastily, 'had some at breakfast this morning and told us how they were made.'

'Here they make with the enchiladas a very special— how you say—sowse?'

'Sauce,' Cass corrected gently.

'Sí, sowse,' he nodded. 'Is made with tomatoes, onion, chilli and tiny spices. Is very, very good. Me, I will have tamale. You know that?'

Cass shook her head.

'Is soft pudding of cornmeal shaped like so,' he cupped his hand, 'and inside, like small lagoon, is rich meat sowse. Is tasting mmm.' He closed his eyes, shaking his head in ecstasy. Then he grinned and patted his prominent belly ruefully. 'I like too much, I think.' He turned to Derek. 'And what is for you, Meestair Prentice? Is also coffee or hot chocolate, sweet rolls, tortillas and fruit conserva.' He waited expectantly.

Derek pulled a face. 'Isn't there any *proper* food?'

Cass's anger, still bubbling beneath her surface calm, erupted again, though she managed to keep her voice low. 'What do you expect? Fish and chips? Caviar and champagne?'

Derek bridled. 'When Ibarra mentioned lunch I thought at least he'd suggest a European restaurant.'

Cass stared at him. She had learned more about him in the past two days than in the whole eighteen months they'd known one another, and what she now saw both saddened and appalled her. 'Perhaps he imagined that as his guests we would wish to experience all aspects of life here.'

'And maybe he had an eye on the expense account,' Derek grumbled.

'We are in *Mexico*,' Cass pointed out, 'this *is* proper food.' She could not help but be aware that Benito must be listening to their exchange. What would he make of it? She was desperately anxious not to cause any more offence. Enough damage had been done already.

'Not with my digestive system in its present state, it isn't,' he grimaced.

'You should have thought of that before you started drinking on the plane,' Cass retorted with unusual bluntness.

Derek looked startled, then his mouth tightened into a thin, white line. 'Lay off, Cass,' he warned. 'My drinking is *my* business. Just because I've said I'll marry you, don't start——'

Benito had been turning his head from one to the other, like a spectator at a tennis match, his normally cheerful face furrowed in concern. But at Derek's words his smile reappeared like the sun after a storm. 'Marry? You and Mees Elliott will marry?'

'Yes.'

'No.'

Cass and Derek spoke simultaneously and Benito's brows arched like half-moons and climbed up his forehead.

Cass closed her eyes. Her thoughts tumbled over one another as she frantically sought escape from the impossible position Derek had put her in.

Yet it was he who came to her rescue. Pressing her fingers with a palm that was warm and damp, Derek tapped the side of his nose with his free hand and winked at Benito. 'It's a secret,' he whispered. 'No one must know yet, not even Miguel, er—*especially* not him.'

'Ah.' Benito nodded, obviously bewildered.

Cass pulled her hand free from its clammy prison as a dark-haired girl in a short-sleeved red dress and white apron came to take their order. Derek must have remembered his instructions to her not to give Miguel the brush-off. Clearly it had dawned on him that an engagement announcement might dampen whatever interest Miguel had in her.

'Will you order for me, Señor Suarez?' Cass prayed that her bright smile hid the apprehension and anger crawling along her nerves. First Derek had attempted to stake his claim on their arrival, calling her his unofficial fiancée, in order to warn Miguel off. Now, realising Miguel's apparent interest in her might be useful in securing a business agreement, he had done an about-face and was demanding she underplay her relationship with him. A relationship which, as far as she was concerned, did not exist at all. *And* she was supposed to go quietly along with whatever he wanted simply because he had agreed to marry her!

Cass swallowed the resentment that rose like gall in

her throat. She was nothing more than a pawn in Derek's game. Yet, for the moment at least, what else could she do? What if Benito did let it slip? She had told Miguel only that morning she had no intention of marrying Derek. Would he still believe her? Or would this latest revelation only confirm in his eyes, especially after that scene in the vault, that she was secretly in league with Derek for underhand or even criminal reasons? It did not bear thinking about. All she could do was hope and pray that Benito would remain silent.

'*Sí*, but of course.' Benito smiled. 'You like some extra tortillas as well? Is made by the wife of the cook, all by hand. No use machines here. Tortillas from machines like rubber.' He screwed his face up at such sacrilege.

'Oh, yes, thank you.' Cass tried to concentrate as Benito spoke to the waitress in rapid Spanish and she scribbled on a little notepad attached to her belt by a long, fine chain.

'I can't face this foreign stuff. I'll have some black coffee, rolls and an omelette,' Derek announced, adding in an undertone, 'if the chef knows what that is.'

Benito's cheerful face fell into lines of puzzlement for a moment. He spoke again to the waitress. She shrugged and nodded, then hurried behind the counter and through a doorway hung with long strands of coloured beads and ribbon, behind which could be heard chattering voices, the crash of pans and the clatter of crockery.

She returned a few moments later with a large tray and set Cass's and Benito's lunch before them, then darted away again.

'You'd better not wait.' Derek's mouth turned down and he looked quickly away from their plates. 'God knows how long it will be before mine arrives.'

As he spoke the girl emerged from the kitchen once more. On her tray, as well as three cups of coffee and a dish of rolls, was a white plate on which steamed the largest fluffiest omelette Cass had ever seen. The girl placed it carefully in front of Derek and stood back, waiting.

'Is all right?' Benito demanded anxiously. 'Is what you want?'

'Yes. Thanks.' Derek prodded it with his knife. 'It looks fine.' He sounded surprised.

'Do you know,' Benito said, using a tortilla to scoop up his gravy, 'the tortilla, he stop a revolution.' Between mouthfuls he explained. 'Many, many years ago the men of Juchitán make fight with the government. Is going to be very bloody war. But President Diaz, he very clever man. He stop the uprise with not one gun fired.'

Cass was intrigued. 'How on earth did he manage that?'

Benito shrugged, his head on one side. 'He put all women in jail. No women, no tortillas. No tortillas, men have no stomach for fight. Revolution over. Simple, no?' He beamed and Cass laughed.

'My wife, when she angry, make threat to me: Benito, you no do this, no tortillas.' He spread his hands eloquently. 'A man must eat.' He leaned a little towards Cass and confided. 'My wife, she very beautiful. We married five years, have two little girls, also very beautiful. Soon she have another baby. I tell her, this time I want a son. She says we have what God gives.' He beamed again. 'Is OK.' His face dropped. 'She no sleep so good. The baby kick all night. So at two o'clock I am making the hot chocolate. Then the baby sleep, my wife sleep, but I no can sleep. Is very hard to have babies.'

Cass nodded and looked quickly down at her plate to hide her smile as she realised the significance of Miguel's conversation with Luisa on their arrival.

Miguel. As Benito began to ask questions about the English climate compared to that of Mexico, Cass replied, but with only half her attention. The rest of her mind was on Miguel.

In the car he had seemed quite deliberately to be pushing back the boundaries of formality, blatantly exploiting the flashes of almost telepathic understanding that crackled between them like an electrical charge. And before that, at breakfast, and even down in the paddock, he had ignored convention, striking with lightning speed and shocking accuracy to the heart of whatever they were discussing.

How different it had been as they left the vault. How cold and unreachable he had looked.

That was yet one more thing she would have to sort out with Derek, exactly what *had* happened.

'I think is time we go back now, yes?' Benito broke into her reverie.

'Yes, of course.' She gave him a bright smile and excused herself for a few moments. In the ladies' room, Cass repaired her lipstick and quickly ran a comb through her thick hair, then stared thoughtfully at her reflection, giving it the same critical appraisal she applied in selecting stones for one of her designs.

Wide-set hazel eyes, fringed with thick, gold-tipped lashes stared back at her. A small nose dusted with freckles between high cheekbones enhanced with a touch of blusher, and a wide, shapely mouth, whose corners had a natural upward tilt, completed the usual complement of features. The chin, with its unexpected air of stubbornness, led to a slender graceful neck about which tumbled glossy chestnut hair.

Cass curled a strand around one finger, her head tilting to one side as a faraway look stole into her eyes. She had learned in childhood to live with remarks concerning the colour of her hair, some flattering, others not, especially when the summer sun lightened it in streaks to dappled auburn. But never, ever had it been compared to a vibrant, shimmering gemstone. A delicious shiver tingled through her. But the memory was overlaid almost immediately by a vision of Miguel's face, closed and unapproachable, as he walked away across the reception area.

Swiftly, she bundled comb and lipstick back into her handbag and turned away from the mirror, ashamed of her thoughts, of the budding hope his interest and attention had nurtured and which, despite her misgivings, stubbornly refused to die.

The afternoon passed quickly. Benito proved a thoughtful and interesting guide. He showed them through each of the four cutting-rooms, pointing out the different types of cutting-discs: brass, copper and tin for harder stones; pewter or lead for softer ones, and little pots of diamond powder, emery and carborundum used as abrasives.

'What you call this in English?' he asked Cass, indicating the flat turntable at which the cutters sat to work.

'A lapidary wheel, I think,' she replied uncertainly, suddenly aware of how little she knew about the origins of the gems with which she worked.

'Wheel now driven by electricity,' he explained, 'but before it have a pedal for the foot.' He showed them wooden discs covered with cloth or leather for polishing.

Cass was fascinated by the gemsticks on to which the cutter cemented a stone then held it against the revolving disc at a chosen angle. To hold his hand steady and guide him from one angle to the next on a faceted stone, the cutter would fix the opposite end of the stick in one of several rows of holes running from top to bottom of a piece of wood shaped like a fat carrot.

'Is called a jamb peg,' Benito said over Cass's shoulder.

'It looks a right cobble-up to me,' Derek observed,

both tone and expression scathing. 'Why doesn't Ibarra modernise? There must be machines that could do the job far more efficiently?'

'Faster, maybe,' Benito allowed. 'We have four such machines, but the men do not like. They say the stones all have different—how you say——' he tutted impatiently and rubbed the material of his sleeve between finger and thumb.

'Texture?' Cass offered.

'Sí, sí,' he beamed in gratitude, 'texture, and a good cutter can sense by touch when is time to change from one angle to another. This not possible with machine. Also machine cannot mend flaw like a man.'

'Mend flaws? Are you kidding?' Derek did not mask his derision.

Benito turned to Cass, puzzled. 'Do I make mistake? My English, he no so good.'

Cass glared at Derek. 'I think Mr Prentice finds it difficult to believe that a flawed stone can be mended, made perfect.'

'Sí, sí,' Benito nodded vigorously. 'Is possible. We do here many times. Is like magic. I watch.'

Cass was fascinated. 'How do they do it?'

'It take much concentrating,' Benito began.

'Do they smoke grass and recite spells?' Derek muttered, plainly bored.

'Will you *shut up*!' Cass hissed at him and turned back to Benito. 'Please go on,' she coaxed. 'You were saying?'

'The cutter must choose very carefully his disc and which abrasive he use. Then he let the disc work dry. This make face of stone hot and when is hot enough it melt, just enough to close up the flaw. It take very great skill to be good cutter. Many, many things to learn. Here we have best in the country. They learn from their fathers and grandfathers.'

'Would you please thank them for allowing us to

watch them work?' Cass asked.

Benito looked delighted and his quick flood of Spanish brought smiles and nods from the cutters, some old with thin, bent bodies and gnarled, corded hands, others young, sporting Zapata moustaches beneath limpid eyes.

They went next to the sorting-room where stones coming in from the rest of the country and abroad were recorded, then divided up for the cutters. But as they entered, Derek announced that he would not accompany them further.

'Fascinating though all this is,' his tone made it clear he found it nothing of the sort, 'I shall have a wander round the town, perhaps do a little shopping.' He flashed Cass a meaningful glance which she ignored. 'I'll be back in an hour or so.' He didn't wait for an answer, marching off down the passage to the security door.

Benito's eyebrows arched into crescents. Cass gave a tiny shrug, which combined resignation, embarrassment and relief.

The next hour gave her the first oppportunity she had ever had to handle the rough chunks of rock and mineral exactly as they had been taken from the ground. It was an absorbing and awesome experience. She mentally compared this raw material, dull and lack-lustre, with the rainbow hues of the beautifully cut and polished gems she handled every day. Recalling the incandescent flame of the magnificent fire opal she could not suppress a small tug of regret. She had never been an acquisitive person; possessions meant little to her. But that stone was something special. How she would have loved to own it. Dragging her thoughts back, she followed Benito along the benches.

There were many different agates, which she already knew were not really stones at all, but fossilised wood and bone which had become opalised. There were lumps of quartz she recognised as amethyst from its colour which ranged over pale lilac, through violet to rich purple; garnets of reddish-brown, cinnamon, wine-purple and crimson bedded in their grey mother-rock. Long, column-shaped crystals of topaz of yellow, sherry-gold and apricot lay next to chunks of colourless rock crystal and turquoise varying from sky-blue to green.

Benito talked and she listened, content merely to put a question now and then. Her respect and liking for the little man was growing by the minute as she recognised the range of his knowledge and his dedication both to his job and to Miguel Ibarra.

Interrupted by an announcement from Luisa over the intercom that there was a phone call for him, Cass glanced at her watch and was amazed to see that it was after five.

Benito escorted her back to reception then took his call at the desk. It was very brief. He approached Cass looking very apologetic.

'Don Miguel, he very sorry, cannot leave yet. I am to take you back to the *hacienda*. He will join you for dinner. Is OK?'

Cass's spirits rose as quickly as they had sunk. 'Thank you, Señor Suarez,' she gave him a dazzling smile, 'that's fine.'

'You call me Benito, is more friendly. If you no mind?' he added hastily, his round face worried.

'I'd be delighted,' she assured him. 'And you call me Cass.'

'Cass?' he repeated. 'Is unusual name.'

'It's Cassandra really,' she explained, 'an ancient Greek name. It means man's helpmate.' She recalled the way it had sounded on Miguel's lips and shivered.

'That a very beautiful name for a lovely and charming

lady.' His gallantry and the blush that darkened his skin touched her.

'Thank you, Benito, but——' her mouth drooped wryly, '—right now I don't think it is very suitable.'

'Please,' he shifted from one foot to the other, twisting his stubby fingers together, 'you no be angry. I say name is right but——' he hesitated, then blurted, 'you choose wrong man.'

Before Cass could make any reply the glass doors hissed softly open and Derek strode in. A carrier bag swung from one hand and from his stance and the evasiveness in his eyes Cass knew at once he had been drinking.

Benito hurried over to explain the new arrangements and Derek patted him clumsily on the shoulder, telling him not to worry, it was no problem.

At least he didn't appear to have had very much. His speech was quite normal and his co-ordination unimpaired. In fact his temper appeared to have improved quite markedly. But when he winked suggestively at Cass, she looked quickly away, knots forming in her stomach as she realised what lay ahead of her.

To her enormous relief Benito suggested they leave at once. She contrived to sit in the front, to Derek's obvious annoyance, but she had no intention of putting Benito in the position of being merely a chauffeur, nor did she wish to give Derek even the slightest encouragement to believe she wanted to be close to him.

She spent the journey with her mind working on two levels. Part of it listened and responded to Benito's conversation, the other part was trying to work out the best way of making it clear to Derek that she would not marry him, now or in the future. Underlying it all was anticipation of seeing Miguel again and her stomach churned with a mixture of longing and dread.

When they arrived, Cass thanked Benito warmly and

while Derek was still getting out of the Range Rover she
sped away to her room, ignoring his shouts.

After a refreshing shower, she dressed with care.
Desperate to boost her confidence she chose one of her
favourite outfits, a sleeveless sheath of cream silk jersey
topped by a batwing-sleeved jacket in chocolate-brown
that tied in a floppy bow on one hip. She slipped her feet
into matching high heels and knew that on the surface at
least she was a picture of cool elegance. She had put her
hair up, securing it with three combs in a pile of loose
curls, to reveal earrings of coral set in gold, one of her
own designs.

She had taken the precaution of locking her door but
still jumped, her heart thumping when Derek knocked
as she had guessed he would, and demanded in
wheedling tones to be let in.

'I'm not quite ready,' she called back, 'but I won't be
long. You go on down.'

He started to argue, but she didn't answer and after a
few moments she heard his footsteps receding along the
passage.

Leaning against the bedstead Cass closed her eyes.
Then taking a deep breath, she added a final touch of
blusher to disguise her nervous pallor. Her make-up
complete, she squared her shoulders and unlocking the
door, went downstairs.

As she reached the hall, Miguel appeared, carrying a
bowl of ice-cubes. He had clearly not had time to
change, for he still wore the pale grey suit she had seen
him in at breakfast.

They both stopped, less than a yard apart. From the
open door leading to the sitting-room came the muted
sound of voices. But Cass was aware only of the furrow
between Miguel's dark brows and the tension in the set
of his mouth.

His black gaze swept over her and she knew not one

detail of her appearance had escaped him, but there was no glimmer of warmth in his eyes.

'I gather congratulations are in order.' Like dry ice his tone chilled and burned at the same time.

For a moment Cass simply stared at him, not understanding what he meant. Then, as one wing-like brow tilted, realisation dawned. She felt nausea rising in her throat. Surely Derek couldn't have—*he wouldn't*— But he had.

'I know it's a woman's privilege to change her mind,' Miguel was saying, his voice seeming far away as she fought the rage that was literally shaking her, 'but I thought you——' He broke off, clearly angry with himself. 'Oh well, no matter,' he said brusquely. 'Allow me to escort you in.'

'Miguel, wait,' she pleaded, her voice low and taut. Hot colour suffused her face as his eyes narrowed at her use of his name. But there was no time to worry about what he would make of that. She had to convince him she had *not* changed her mind, that Derek had spoken without her knowledge or her consent. 'Please listen——' But she got no further.

'Miguel, darling, what *are* you doing?' A bell-like female voice floated towards them and Cass's head flew round.

Framed in the doorway stood a girl of twenty or twenty-one with midnight-black hair braided into a coronet on top of her head. Her long-sleeved dress, a frothy confection in fuchsia-pink with a flounced skirt, had a low V-neckline exposing gleaming golden skin and the deep valley between her voluptuous breasts. 'The ice will be melting,' she accused, her pouting mouth painted the same vivid colour as her dress. 'I can't imagine why you didn't ring for one of the servants to get it.'

Her dark eyes were dramatically made up, outlined in

black and shaded with pink, lilac and gold shadow. As they lighted on Cass they underwent a subtle change, and Cass sensed herself examined and assessed with lightning speed.

The girl swayed provocatively towards them and linked her arm through Miguel's. 'So it is *you* we are hearing so much about.' Her voice was soft and throaty and her lips drew back from small, white teeth in a polite, cold smile. 'I am Teresa, Miguel's betrothed.'

CHAPTER FIVE

CASS'S eyes flew to Miguel but his expression was glacial. Deeply shaken, first by Derek's action and now by the introduction of a fiancée at whose existence Miguel had not even hinted, Cass had only her pride to fall back on. Self-respect demanded she conceal her double shock and the sudden, wrenching pain, all the more savage for being totally unexpected.

'You must forgive me,' she forced a smile, meeting Teresa's appraising stare, and marvelling at the level voice issuing from her own lips, 'I had no idea Derek intended to make such an announcement this evening.' From the corner of her eye she saw a brief flicker crack Miguel's impassivity. She could not bring herself to mouth the conventional phrases. She was *not* pleased to meet Teresa. 'H-how do you do?'

Teresa inclined her head regally, but made no move to shake hands. It was a clear snub but Cass's control did not falter. Obviously Teresa was not overjoyed to see her either.

Cass looked once more at Miguel, hearing her own voice as if from a distance. 'Your assistant was most generous with his time and knowledge. I very much enjoyed our tour of the cutting-rooms and I certainly learned a lot.'

His only acknowledgement was a nod, but curiosity vied with cynicism in his hooded eyes.

Cass's nails dug deeply into her palms. She could not bear this a moment longer. Could she plead a headache? Even as the thought occurred she dismissed it. On no account must Miguel Ibarra be allowed to believe that his betrothal made the slightest difference to her.

The sound of Derek's voice raised in laughter drifted from the sitting-room. To whom was he talking? How many more people had she yet to meet? In their eyes tonight was a celebration. Derek had announced his forthcoming marriage to her. *Why had he done it?*

Her own sense of privacy and awareness of her responsibility as a guest made it impossible simply to deny his claim. To do so would brand him a fool and a liar, and though he deserved it, she knew her action would invoke sympathy for *him*, not her. Never had she been more acutely aware of the advantages of being a man.

She had no choice but to walk into the sitting-room with a smile plastered on to her face, to make the appropriate small talk and, later, to eat, even though her stomach had tensed into a small, hard knot and the thought of food was revolting.

A shaft of white-hot anger pierced the blackness that threatened to overwhelm her. She nursed it, fanned it, clung to it. To hell with Derek and his devious plans, and to hell with Miguel Ibarra and his centrefold girl-friend!

She was her own woman. They would not drive her into a corner like some wounded animal. She had an excellent reason for being here—her work. She would concentrate on that and exclude everything else.

'And did Mr Prentice match your enjoyment in learning about the practical side of our business?' Miguel's sardonic question told Cass he already knew the answer.

'You will have to ask him,' she replied. 'I have decided to make a point of not speaking for anyone else. It is too easy to be mistaken, even about people one thinks one knows well.' Then with her head high, conscious of her heightened colour under the sudden gleam in his eyes, she moved past them both to the open door. Somewhere

at the back of her mind a little voice told her somethin
wasn't quite right. She gave herself a mental shake. *Non*
of this was right. It was all a hopeless mess. But she ha
to brave it out for the time being.

As she entered the room Derek excused himself from
the man he was talking to and came quickly to her side
He grasped her hands and under the pretence of kissin
her cheek muttered, 'There wasn't any time to war
you. The moment I saw Teresa I knew we'd have t
change our tactics.' Leaving her more confused an
furious than ever, he held her at arm's length. 'Darling
you look absolutely ravishing,' he said loudly, then sli
one arm around her shoulders and with lips that smelle
of whisky pressed another wet kiss to her temple.

Cass steeled herself not to flinch. Her cheek muscle
were beginning to ache from holding her smile in place

Gently disentangling himself from Teresa's posses
sive hold, Miguel came over and took Cass's free hand
His fingers were strong and hard and his touch was
high-voltage shock as his thumb pressed her knuckle
with what seemed unnecessary force. 'Come, I wi
introduce you to Teresa's parents.' It was a command

Derek released her with an exaggerated show c
reluctance, but turned at once to Teresa, showering he
with lavish compliments. Teresa revelled in this atten
tion, purring with pleasure, apparently heedless c
Miguel's reaction.

Wondering exactly how he did feel, Cass glanced u
quickly and was surprised to see, instead of anger o
jealousy, mild exasperation clouding his strong feature
But when he turned back to her his expression hardene
and a cold hand clutched at her heart.

Teresa's obvious rebuff still smarted and Cass was o
the point of asking what made him think Teresa'
parents would want to meet *her*, but stifled the impulse
'How nice,' she said coolly, staring ahead to avoid hi

eyes, and sensed rather than saw his sharp look.

Cass felt as though she were walking on jelly as Miguel led her towards the couple talking quietly in front of the button-back sofa of mahogany-coloured leather. His touch reawakened all the attraction she felt towards him. She tried to ease her fingers free but, as if divining her intention, his grip was already tightening. Short of snatching her hand away, a move guaranteed to attract attention, not to mention curiosity, both of which would rebound on *her*, she could do nothing.

Trying to control her quickening breath as her pulses raced, she knew he must be aware of her tension and the tremors she was unable to control. She prayed he would put it all down to nervousness and the shock of Derek's surprise announcement.

She was suddenly conscious of being scrutinised by a pair of deep-set, piercingly blue eyes almost on a level with her own. In his dark suit Teresa's father appeared slim, almost wiry, and his bearing was proud. Silvering hair was cut short and brushed back and a small, military-looking moustache adorned a long upper lip. Only his skin, deeply lined and leathery, gave any clue to his age which Cass guessed was in the mid-fifties.

'Señor Morelos, Señora.' Miguel bowed briefly towards the woman who stood slightly behind her husband and resembled a faded, dried flower in her plain dress of muted colours. 'Permit me to introduce Miss Cassandra Elliott.'

He released her hand, offering it, still marked by the pressure of his grip, to Teresa's father who caught it lightly and raised it to his lips.

Cass felt a faint tickling sensation as the bristly moustache brushed against her fingers. '*Buenas tardes, señor, señora.*' She shook the limp hand Teresa's mother held out.

'*Ah*,' Señor Morelos's blue eyes sharpened. '*¿Habla usted Español?*'

Cass shook her head. 'Very little, I'm afraid, though I find it a very beautiful language to listen to.'

'I think we must wish you much happiness, no? On your betrothal?' Señor Morelos's English was heavily accented and though his face creased in a smile his eyes remained watchful.

His words jolted Cass, an after-shock to the original blow. But she was saved from having to reply by the major-domo's arrival to announce dinner and the general exodus towards the door.

Cass hung back, wanting a moment to herself, trying to fathom the expression she had glimpsed in Teresa's father's eyes. It had been more than polite interest. There had been critical curiosity and something else, *unease*? That was ridiculous. What possible threat could she pose to him?

'You have had nothing to drink.' Miguel's voice, just above her left ear, made her jump. 'Would you like something to take in with you?'

'No, thank you.' Her calm reply betrayed none of the upheaval within.

'I see our respective fiancés are finding much of mutual interest.' There was a quality in his voice, a quiet but unmistakable irony, that brought Cass's head round quickly. She sensed deeper shades of meaning and, as she met his dark gaze and watched one wing-like brow lift, she felt her colour deepen.

'As a conscientious host you must be delighted,' she retorted lightly.

'Oh I am.' His tone was dry. 'But as a conscientious host I would not care to see one of my guests made jealous by the behaviour of certain others.'

'Please do not concern yourself on *my* account,' she responded sharply, 'jealousy is not an emotion I am familiar with.' She could have bitten her tongue out. She realised with icy clarity what she had said wasn't true. Two days ago it would have been. But now? Tonight, for the first time in her life, she had felt jealousy's sharp fangs and was helpless in their grip.

'I find that strange,' Miguel murmured, looking deep into her eyes. 'You claim to be an artist——'

'I do not *claim*,' Cass interrupted hotly. 'I *am*.'

'An artist?' he queried softly. 'A creature of mood, of passion and temperament? Denying one of the most fundamental of all emotions?' His eyes narrowed. 'To accept that I would have to believe you have never loved.'

Cass shrugged, her face aflame. 'Believe what you like.' She turned away but he caught her arm, his grasp tight and painful.

'If you are not in love,' his voice was low and harsh, 'why the announcement? Why are you engaged?'

'Why are *you*?' she flared back, knowing as the words flew from her lips that this was what had been gnawing at her just below the surface of her mind. The signs had been visible and she had seen them, but their meaning had been obscured by her own two-fold shock. Even allowing for his habit of masking his thoughts and feelings, not once had he touched or looked at Teresa, his own fiancée, with anything resembling love.

His shock was plain in the tightening of his mouth and the sudden bleakness in his eyes as they stared at one another. The air between them was charged and Cass gasped softly as Miguel jerked her towards him.

'Cass?' Derek stuck his head around the door. 'You're holding everyone up again.' His slightly bloodshot eyes flicked suspiciously from one to the other. Miguel released her arm, dropping his hands to his side.

'I'm sorry,' she said automatically, lowering her eyes as she fingered the sleeve of her jacket, not sure for which of them she intended the apology. She started across the hall, still conscious of the bruising imprint of Miguel's grip.

'No problem, is there?' Derek muttered as she walked ahead of him into the dining-room, acutely aware of Miguel only a pace or two behind.

'Oh, no.' Her terse irony was completely lost on Derek and he nodded, smiling with satisfaction.

She slid on to the chair he held out for her, not realising until she was seated that he had placed himself next to Teresa and her next to Miguel. What was he up to now? she wondered. Then, as the tightness at the back of her skull began to encircle her head, she abandoned all attempts to think. She was mentally and emotionally exhausted.

She tried to concentrate solely on the meal, which looked delicious. In the centre of the table stood bowls of fried sweetcorn with peppers and mushrooms, a large dish of green salad, prawns in garlic, freshly made tomato sauce and an avocado dip, all to be eaten with tacos or tortillas. Everyone helped themselves, passing the bowls around as Miguel filled their glasses from an earthenware pitcher with punch which, according to Teresa, was made from orange juice, soda water, limes, tonic and tequila.

She described the ingredients of each dish to Derek with great vivacity as she tempted him with morsels from her own plate. Cass watched him eat, wryly recalling his rejection of Mexican food in the restaurant that very lunchtime.

Cass herself managed to fend off questions regarding her wedding plans with smiling evasions, while Derek patted her hand, her shoulder and anything else he could reach, the alcohol he had consumed making him clumsy and loud. She was burningly aware of Miguel's eyes on her, eyes she dared not meet. She toyed with her food, pushing it around her plate in a pretence of eating.

The main course was Chilli con Carne and the punch was set aside by all except Derek in favour of clear spring water topped with ice-cubes. Finally, Consuelo brought in a fruit salad comprising strawberries, fresh pineapple, guavas, mango and melon, served with tiny circles of shortbread.

Cass managed a few mouthfuls but it was like sawdust in her mouth as she answered Señor Morelos's questions about her work. It was a little while before she realised his reactions were critical, almost disapproving.

As her confusion grew she glanced at Miguel, seeking clarification and, though she hated to admit it, reassurance. Had she offended in some way?

'Señor Morelos is modern in his outlook concerning the development of our country,' Miguel explained, his dark eyes gleaming, 'but less so concerning the place of women in society.'

'But surely,' Cass ventured, 'one depends upon the other?'

'I have tried to express this view to Teresa,' Miguel said mildly. 'It did occur to me she might like to do more with her life than be a decorative hostess.'

'But I shall do more, *querido*,' Teresa purred, 'I shall be the mother of your sons; what could be more demanding or fulfilling than that?' She flashed him a triumphant smile.

Cass laid down her spoon with infinite care, feeling as though she had been kicked in the stomach. The images Teresa's words conjured so vividly in her over-wrought imagination were painful beyond belief and she shied away from them, resolutely blanking her mind.

'I was thinking of the present and the more immediate future,' Miguel replied coolly. He turned once more to Cass. 'In Mexico it is not considered complimentary to praise a woman's intelligence. Her beauty, yes. Indeed, all girls are brought up to consider themselves beautiful, and who is to say that is wrong? Which child is not beautiful in its mother's eyes? But to call a woman clever, while not exactly an insult, is not considered polite as it is also an affront to a man's machismo.'

Cass's eyes widened. 'How on earth does that follow?'

'What does it matter? You must just accept that it is so, Miss Elliott,' Teresa's clear, imperious tones cut in. 'It is a man's duty to provide and protect. A woman seeking to do those things for herself challenges the status of men. She insults them.'

'But I——' Cass began, only for Teresa to interrupt again.

'Argument is not feminine. A woman's role is to please her man with her beauty, to run his home and to bear his children. If you are unfortunate enough to need to work because you have no money or no man to care for you, it is best spoken of lightly or not at all. Far better to consider it a misfortune to be ignored as far as possible and devote your efforts to encouraging the gentler, less competitive side of your nature.'

Cass was dumbfounded. She could see the girl really believed what she was saying. It was not deliberate malice, merely the code by which she had been brought up.

But she *loved* her work, it was an expression of her innermost self. Never in a million years could she consider it 'unfortunate'. Then she thought of the almost continuous conflict that had existed between herself and Miguel. They had done little since her arrival *except* argue. Did *he* think her unfeminine? Before she could prevent it her eyes sought his and read in their black depths amusement. *He knew what she was thinking.*

A blush warmed her throat and coloured her face as she looked quickly down at her plate. What did it matter what he thought? He was nothing to her. How could he be? He was engaged to someone else, a girl of his own country, his own culture and background. A girl who had been brought up to believe that a woman's sole purpose in life was to find, win and keep a man. Someone who had never needed or wanted to work and had little interest in women who did. *A girl whom, despite all this, he did not love and who, notwithstanding her air of possessiveness, was openly flirting with a man who had just announced his own engagement.*

Suddenly Cass had had enough. Señor Morelos was watching her with something akin to suspicion, while his wife, who had hardly spoken during the meal, toyed with the remains of her fruit salad. Teresa, having dismissed Cass's hard-won and much loved career as something to be ashamed of, had returned her interest to Derek, giving him languorous side-long glances as she murmured remarks that only he could hear while refilling their glasses with punch. He was preening under her attentions and, emboldened by the alcohol, had twice leaned over to whisper in the small, pink ear from which dangled an opal and diamond earring, the milky stone flashing its iridescence with each toss of her dark head.

The opal reminded Cass of the moments in the vault before the alarm had gone off, of her enjoyment and interest, of the growing attraction and many-layered conversation she had shared with the man who now regarded her, his haughty features impassive, with the sharp clear gaze of an eagle.

'Please excuse me,' she murmured hoarsely, her chair scraping noisily on the cool tiles as she stood up. 'I'm so sorry—a headache.'

Derek looked round in surprise, but Miguel was already half-way to his feet.

'No,' she blurted, half pleading, and hurried out into the hall, almost colliding with the major-domo who was carrying a large silver tray laden with coffee-pot, milk jug and sugar bowl and tiny gold-rimmed cups and saucers.

Cass mumbled an apology and sped up the stairs, not stopping until she reached the sanctuary of her own room, and turned the key.

Sinking down on to the bed she rested her forehead against the cool brass rail. 'Today holds much for you,' Miguel had said at breakfast that morning. He certainly had a gift for understatement. Cass tried to smile and choked on a sob instead. She could never have dreamed how much could happen or how ridiculously bruised she would feel.

She had been wrong about so many things, particularly Derek. She didn't know what to believe any more. She hardly recognised the man she thought she knew. And what of Miguel? Her intuition had told her that his betrothal to Teresa was no love match. Or was that, too, just wishful thinking?

She closed her eyes, and to her horrified surprise hot tears seeped through her lashes and slid down her cheeks. Furiously she dashed them away. She must still be suffering the effects of altitude and jet-lag.

Quickly wiping her wet face with the back of her hand, Cass undressed and put her clothes carefully away. She hugged the soft folds of the jade velour robe over her cotton nightie and stood in front of the mirror to remove the remaining traces of make-up. Her eyes were hot and her skin felt drawn and tight.

While she was in the bathroom bathing her face with cold water, there was a knock on the door.

Immediately tense again, she straightened up, pressing the towel to her cheeks. She did not want to talk to anyone, yet not to answer would be ill-mannered and might give cause for concern. There was a second knock, slightly louder.

Tossing the towel on to the rail she re-entered the bedroom. 'Who is it?' she called reluctantly.

'Consuelo, *señorita*,' came the reply.

Vastly relieved not to hear Derek's voice or that of Miguel, Cass quickly unlocked the door. The housekeeper handed her a small tray on which stood a mug of hot, frothy chocolate and a white envelope.

'Señor Ibarra send,' Consuelo said in thick, heavily accented English, frowning with effort. 'He say you no eat so this help you sleep.' She turned away.

'*Muchas gracias*,' Cass called after her and, relocking the door, placed the mug carefully on the bedside cabinet. She picked up the envelope with mingled curiosity and unease, tossing the tray to the bottom of the bed.

The thick white sheet of paper crackled as she unfolded it. In bold black scrawl the message was brief. '6 a.m. M.'

Cass stared at it, uncomprehending. Then her heart leapt into her throat. He had invited—no, commanded—her to ride into the hills with him at dawn to watch the sunrise. And she, piqued at his tone, had accepted. This was a reminder.

Sinking down on the bed, Cass sipped the cinnamon-flavoured chocolate, enjoying its smooth richness and feeling its warmth ease loose the knots in her stomach. What a mass of contradictions he was. He had noticed her lack of appetite and had arranged for a hot drink to be sent up. Yet he had made no effort to stop Teresa and her father denigrating her beliefs and her career. Was the drink simply the mark of a conscientious host, or had he understood how upset she was?

Cass shook her head and, suddenly restless, began to pace the room. She looked at the note again. It could hardly have said less. The day's events had pushed the arrangement right out of her mind. But not, it seemed, his.

Doubts crowded in. Should she go? The 'invitation' had been more of a challenge, a gauntlet tossed down for her to ignore or pick up as she chose. Yet the very act of accepting his challenge had altered their relationship. After their initial clash his response towards her had been markedly different. Certainly it was not simply because she was a woman. As Derek had made so very clear, a man with Miguel Ibarra's wealth, position and good looks would be fighting women off, not having to search for them. Was that what Teresa was? A shield to keep other women at bay? Cass pondered the idea then abruptly dismissed it. He was not a man to hide behind a woman's skirts. Whatever the real reason for his engagement and, judging by his exasperated expression, the relationship held as many problems as pleasures, it was not an escape.

Cass placed the empty mug on the tray and set it down on the chest of drawers. She looked at the note once more, then raised her eyes to her reflection in the mirror. Her colour was high and her eyes fever-bright.

She had a choice. She could avoid him, maintaining the new distance between them by refusing to go. Or she could take the opportunity to explain. That was the more honest thing to do. It was also the more dangerous. She was drawn to him. No man had ever affected her the way he did and spending time in his company could only increase that attraction. Yet under no circumstances could she afford to reveal her feelings. He was not free and it had to be because he chose it so. He was not a man to be manipulated. To reveal even a hint of the fascination he held for her would invite—what? Amusement? Irritation? *Or contempt.*

She bit her lip, made her decision, and went to the bathroom to clean her teeth.

Ready for bed, she switched off the light then, obeying an impulse, drew back the curtains and looked out on to the moonwashed garden below. There was not a breath of wind. The trees stood like black sentinels, their branches raised in silent homage to the night.

The moon was behind the house out of sight, but in its silvery light Cass could see quite clearly the paved drive and the paddock fence.

A dark figure moved from the veranda on to the flags, half-turning to cup his hands round a flaring match as he paused to light a small cigar. The momentary brightness illuminated high, flat cheekbones and a curved Aztec nose.

Watching Miguel, Cass's heart kicked. He was totally relaxed, his feet slightly apart, one hand in his pocket as the other raised the cigar to his lips. She caught the faint fragrance of smoke.

He gave the impression of a successful man enjoying a few moments' quiet contemplation before sleeping. But Cass already knew enough about him to recognise that appearances could be cruelly deceptive. Was he really as tranquil as he seemed? Or was he, behind hooded gleaming eyes, as confused and perplexed as she? For one fierce moment she hoped so. She had not sought any of this. Much of the responsibility was his.

He puffed on the cigar once more. Cass stepped back, her emotions muddled and painful, and lifted her arms to close the curtains again. A movement below caught her eye and she saw Teresa, a silver fox fur coat covering her dress and framing her elegant head, glide across the flags to rest one white hand on his shoulder.

Miguel glanced round. Teresa was very close, her head tilted back, her white teeth glistening in the moonlight. Pressing herself against him she raised her other hand to trail enamelled nails down his cheek, then pulled his head down to hers. Cass saw him toss the cigar away. Quickly lowering her head to shut out the scene she closed the curtains. But her imagination rolled on, giving her no peace.

As she turned to slip into bed she heard two pairs of footsteps in the passage outside, and muted voices speaking Spanish. A door opened and closed. Clearly Teresa and her parents were staying the night. *But where would Teresa be sleeping?*

Cass pulled the cold sheet over her and half turned to punch the pillow viciously. *It was none of her business.* She lay on her back, shivering, and was glad of the small discomfort. It helped take her mind off what she had witnessed out in the moonlight and its all too obvious conclusion.

A muffled thump not far from her bedroom door, followed by a string of curses, stopped her breath in her throat.

She listened intently, her fingers curling into her palms. It could only be Derek. He had clearly ignored her advice about cutting back on alcohol.

She stared at the door, her nerves tightening as the sounds drew nearer. Please let him go by. She repeated the words silently, over and over, willing him to go on past and into his own room.

The crash of his shoe against her door gave her a violent start.

'Cass,' he demanded against the wood, 'wanna talk to you.' He tried the handle, quietly at first, then rattling it angrily as he realised the door was locked. 'C'mon, open it will you?' His voice was growing louder, more impatient. 'Wassa matter with you? We're engaged, dammit.'

Cass's teeth were clenched so hard her jaw ached. What should she do? If she didn't open the door he would disturb the entire household. But if she did——

'C'mon, Cassie,' he wheedled, 'let me in. You don't

have to be shy with me.' He began to sing, 'I've got something for you,' but it ended abruptly on a hiccup.

Kicking off the covers, Cass padded across to the door but did not touch it. 'Please, Derek,' she begged, 'go back to your room. I'll see you in the morning.'

'Aaah, so you are awake.' His voice was loud and slurred, sounding both pleased and irritated. 'C'mon now, stop teasing and open this door.'

'*Go away!*' She whispered fiercely.

'Not until you kiss me goodnight.'

Cass wiped damp palms down the sides of her nightdress.

'I'm entitled to that, for God's sake.' He was shouting now, his tone ugly. 'I've kept my part of the bargain, now you damn well keep yours. I'm not going to be messed around like this. I'm fed up with the hands-off treatment. There's a word for girls like you. Now open this bloody door or I'll kick it down!'

Rubbing the tops of her icy arms, Cass bit her lip so hard she tasted blood. Feet pounded up the stairs two at a time and overwhelming relief left her legs trembling as she heard Miguel's voice. He sounded perfectly calm and not even out of breath.

'I think you have mistaken your room, Mr Prentice. Your door is on the other side of the passage.'

The silence seemed interminable. Then Teresa's clear voice, full of mingled curiosity and annoyance, demanded to know why Miguel had suddenly raced away without a word, and what was going on. No one answered her. Cass didn't even breathe. She could almost hear Derek's fuddled brain debating whether to tell Miguel to mind his own business thereby risking irreparable damage to his hopes of a contract, or to hang on to his temper and take the way out that had been offered.

Eventually he muttered, 'Oh yeah? How'd I manage

that then?' and Cass let her breath out in a long, shuddering sigh. ''s easy to get lost in a place this size,' Derek said truculently.

'I'm sure it won't happen a second time.' Miguel's voice was an unsheathed blade. 'But should you need anything, my room is just across the passage from yours, and I'm a very light sleeper.' The warning was crystal clear.

Derek grunted and a few moments later Cass heard a door slam. She leaned against the wall, weak and shaken as reaction set in. A light tap on her door made her jump. 'Everything all right?' Miguel's query was more polite than concerned.

'Y-yes,' she stammered. 'Thank you.'

'*De nada,*' came the dry reply. 'Sleep well.'

As Cass pushed herself away from the wall her mouth softened in a shaky smile. '*De nada,*' she repeated to herself, mimicking him. 'It's nothing.'

She heard Teresa murmur something in a coaxing tone. Miguel replied briefly. A staccato click of heels and a slammed door told their own story. Then the door next to hers closed.

Cass climbed wearily back into bed. Excitement was all very well, but today had contained enough to last her a lifetime.

A few moments later she heard a shower running. She sat up with a jerk, staring wide-eyed towards her open bathroom door, then realised that Miguel's en suite bathroom must adjoin her own.

Lying back she stared at the ceiling and listened to him humming to himself as he showered. It was an extraordinarily intimate sound.

Cass's lashes fluttered down. Miguel had warned Derek off and he was not sharing his bed with Teresa that night.

She slept.

CHAPTER SIX

IT WAS still dark when Cass stepped out into the passage the following morning. Dressed in warm stretch pants and a thick sweater over a fine wool shirt, she had brushed her hair back into a loose pony-tail to keep it out of the way.

Holding her boots in one hand, she closed her door with great care then leapt a foot into the air as a hand descended on her shoulder.

'Ssshh,' Miguel warned softly, placing his fingers gently over her lips.

Her heart hammered in her throat, its speed only partly due to the shock he had given her. The warm, light touch on her mouth heightened all her senses and set her nerves quivering.

'You frightened me,' she whispered shakily, hoping he would accept that explanation for the trembling that shook her.

'Not possible,' he breathed close to her ear, adding drily, 'your imagination does a better job than I ever could.'

Giving her no time to respond, he clasped her hand and tugged her towards the stairs. He too was carrying his boots and was wearing the cream breeches and yellow sweater she had seen him in the previous day. Suddenly Cass was overcome by a fit of giggles.

'Quiet!' Miguel warned and pulled her faster down the sweeping staircase. As he reached the bottom he spun round and they collided. She was on the last step and their heads were level.

'What's the matter?' he demanded in a whisper.

Cass shook her head, biting her lips to contain the laughter born of nervous tension and excitement. 'It's ridiculous,' she spluttered. 'This is *your* house, yet we're sneaking about like a couple of criminals.'

He shrugged, his teeth flashing briefly in the dimness. 'This is a very special part of my day. I value it highly and have no wish to share it with people incapable of appreciating what it means to me.'

As she followed him out into the chill grey dawn, his words echoing and re-echoing in her mind, a warm glow spread through Cass. She tried to control it, to play it down. But, like steam from a boiling kettle, it would not be contained and surged like heady wine along her veins. *He was sharing it with her*.

She opened and closed doors for Miguel as he fetched the tack and saddled the horses. Then they mounted up. Miguel led on the chestnut stallion and she followed on a beautiful thoroughbred mare. They wound their way down the path under the oaks, across the dew-soaked grass, and up a winding track into the hills.

The only sounds were the creak of leather and the crunching of the horses' hooves on the stony path. Even the birds had not yet woken.

The stallion's stride quickened and he broke into an easy canter. The mare followed suit and, all of a sudden, Cass was filled with a wonderful sense of well-being.

The mare's superb condition and collected power were evident in her effortless speed. Her mouth was velvet-soft and she responded instantly to the lightest touch on the rein. The cold air felt like champagne on Cass's skin.

Miguel glanced over his shoulder. 'All right?'

'Fantastic!' she called back, her smile totally uninhibited as she revelled in a joyous new sensation of freedom.

For an instant he appeared startled, then his own face creased in a grin that made his dark eyes gleam and deepened the lines bracketting his chiselled mouth.

Leaning forward in the saddle, Miguel gave the stallion its head and the magnificent animal leapt forward, its hooves flying over the dirt.

'Come on, girl,' Cass murmured to the mare, 'they're not going to get away with that.' The mare's ears pricked up and, without further urging, she lengthened her stride, increasing her pace.

The sky was growing lighter by the minute. The all-pervading grey had given way to pearl, pale green and, just above the eastern horizon, primrose.

Pounding along the track they rounded a bend, crossed a high valley and started up a trail that curved round the side of a steep hill.

Glancing skyward once more, Cass saw wraiths of cloud change from oyster to pale pink.

As they reached the far side of the hill, Miguel pulled the stallion to a slithering halt. The mare slowed of her own accord.

Miguel jumped down and held both arms up towards Cass. 'Quick, never mind the reins, let them fall. The horses are trained to stand if the reins are on the ground.'

Throwing her leg over the saddle, Cass slid down into his waiting arms. Her heart contracted and his expression tightened as he held her against him for a brief moment. Releasing her, he seized her hand and pulled her, at a run, several yards further along the trail. Then he stopped and, standing behind her with both hands on her shoulders, turned her sideways.

They were facing a gap between two hills, beyond and below which the highlands stretched into the distance.

'I had no idea we were so high,' Cass panted, still trying to catch her breath.

Miguel squeezed her shoulders gently. 'Ssshh,' he murmured. 'Watch.'

She could feel his chest against her back and his warm

breath on her neck and cheek. Her blood fizzed with exhilaration. Folding her arms, trying to control her leaping awareness of him, so close, *so very close*, she gazed towards the eastern horizon where the whole sky blushed deep rose.

As they watched, the colour changed to coral, then tangerine, then molten gold as the rim of the sun climbed with slow majesty above the farthest hill. The dazzling rays fell upon the mist in the valleys, dissolving it, burning it away.

As the whole shimmering disc rose into the sky, Cass felt a lump in her throat, yet wasn't sure why. The pastel shades of dawn had been banished by this harsh new brilliance. It brought with it a flash of insight that made her catch her breath.

'Tell me,' Miguel said quietly, turning her towards him, reminding her once more of the acute perception that existed between them. His dark eyes held hers, demanding the truth, so she gave it.

'I was just imagining what it must have been like for the Aztec high priest, waiting each morning to greet the sun. Never being *absolutely* sure that it would rise, perhaps appalled by the slaughter of children and ritual blood sacrifice, but too terrified of the consequences *not* to perform them.' She broke off, suddenly embarrassed, and glanced down, her thick lashes veiling her eyes. 'I'm not usually given to melodrama.'

He said nothing. His grip on her shoulders tightened slightly.

Suddenly she wanted him to understand what she had glimpsed. 'I mean—we take so much for granted now, how long a sun will last, what happens when a star goes nova. Our knowledge of astronomy and physics is so vast and complex it's hard to imagine how terrifying it must have been for people who went to sleep each night not sure there would even *be* a tomorrow.'

He cupped her head between his hands. There was a light of triumph in his eyes. 'Now do you know why I asked you to come with me this morning?' he demanded.

'You didn't *ask* me,' Cass demurred, 'it was a cross between a challenge and a command.'

'But you came,' he pointed out.

'Yes.'

'Are you glad?'

'Oh, yes.' Her reply was instant and heartfelt.

'Why?'

'Because it was beautiful and because I think I understand the significance sunrise has for you. Where a Catholic might go to early mass, you come here.' Cass spoke without reserve. Later, when they returned to the *hacienda*, to the pressures and people, and this exquisite clarity was blurred, she might regret opening her heart. But now, at this moment, nothing else mattered.

'You think I am a pagan?' There was a note of amusement in his deep voice as with gentle fingers he brushed tendrils from her forehead and temple.

'You are many things,' she said thoughtfully. All the problems that so beset her yesterday were for the moment forgotten. The barren hillside, the sunrise and Miguel were all that existed. She smiled at him. 'I think there is a part of you which belongs to the old ways.'

He ran his fingers down her cheek and throat, his eyes narrowing, becoming smoky.

Cass swallowed. His touch, so light yet so intimate, ignited a slow-burning fire deep within her that spread its warmth along every nerve. 'Wh-who was she, Miguel?' Cass's throat was dry and her voice sounded husky. 'The Aztec woman?'

'What difference does it make?' His tone was preoccupied, as though his thoughts were on something other than his ancestry.

'None at all. I'm just curious,' Cass smiled. 'I've never known anyone with so direct a link with the past. You have to admit it was a very ... *vivid* period.'

His shoulders moved in an almost imperceptible shrug. 'She was the daughter of the emperor and one of his slave women. There was no stigma attached to such births then. She was acknowledged to be of Royal blood, taught to read, write and speak several languages. And yet,' he paused, one dark brow lifting cynically, 'my mother's family, who were of pure Spanish descent, did not want her to marry my father because of his "tainted" blood.'

Cass gazed up at the proud face above her. The imperious, sculpted features revealed nothing but she sensed a deep anger. 'Your mother obviously had the courage to make her own decision,' she said softly, knowing expressions of outrage or condemnation on her part were not sought, nor would they be welcome. He was stating a fact, not seeking sympathy.

'It cost her dear.'

'Did she ever regret it?'

His voice softened. 'No. She is with him now at the Heart Institute. In fact, it will be interesting to see if the doctors manage to keep her out of the operating theatre.'

'Then whatever the cost, for her it was clearly worth while.'

As he gazed down into her eyes, his brief smile faded, and a brooding intensity darkened his expression. 'And you, Cassandra,' he murmured, 'who are you?'

She shivered suddenly. It was as though all the warmth had gone from the morning. Yet the sun still blazed from a clear, sapphire sky. 'I—I'm not sure any more.'

'You will find out while you are here.' He nodded slowly and there was a strange certainty in his words

She tried to smile. Already so much had changed. 'Is that a threat?'

He drew her towards him and buried one hand in her hair as the other slid down her back and tightened around her waist, effectively imprisoning her. 'A promise,' he whispered and his head came down towards hers.

Cass's hands flew upward in a reflex action to fend him off. 'No,' she croaked, her throat parched, her heart pounding with mingled fear and longing.

'Now you are not honest, *querida*,' he chided, 'with me or with yourself.' Still he held her, neither tightening his hold nor loosening it. His cheek was warm and stubbly against her temple and his hard muscled body drew her like a magnet, promising a bewitching mixture of comfort, new strength and intoxicating excitement. Her confusion was unbearable.

'Honesty is all very well.' Her voice wavered as, like a tidal wave, all the problems and pressures she had left behind reared up, ready to engulf her once more.

'We must pay our dues.' He brushed aside her hesitancy. 'The sun has risen, we have another day.' His smile made her heart turn over. 'I do not demand your heart's blood, merely a kiss.'

Cass's gaze dropped to his mouth, only inches from hers. But her protest died unuttered, for how could she tell him her fear that the one kiss so lightly, teasingly demanded, could all too easily cost her her heart.

Interpreting her silence as acquiescence, a faint smile lifted the corners of his mouth, then his lips brushed hers, as delicately as a moth's wing, once, twice, a third time.

Cass's eyes closed and her fingers curled, gripping his sweater, she could feel the drumbeat of his heart and his body's heat through the thick wool.

Sensing the change, Miguel's mouth captured hers.

She stopped fighting both herself and him and relaxed, letting herself float free on the swirling tide rising inside her. His lips moved with subtle, tantalising expertise, coaxing a response that Cass could not help but give.

As the kiss lengthened, deepened, she vaguely heard his breathing quicken. Her own heart was threatening to burst from her body. She felt light-headed, and a strange, sweet weakness pervaded her.

When at last Miguel lifted his head it was a bereavement, and an involuntary moan escaped her swollen lips.

He held her hard against his taut length and her head fell forward against his shoulder. He was breathing hard and fast and she sensed a battle raging within him.

As reality returned, intrusive and unwelcome, Cass felt unaccountably shy. It was all so bewildering. In conventional terms she barely knew this man. She had met him, and instantly disliked him, only two days before. Yet there was an inexplicable bond between them, a perception and insight neither could truthfully deny. But what did it mean? What would be its effect on their lives?

'Cassandra?' he spoke softly against her hair and she felt the sound vibrate in his throat and chest.

She raised her head. His expression as he looked down at her held both tenderness and resolve.

'It is time to go back.'

'Of course.' She drew away, trying at once to pretend that nothing of any significance had occurred, that this was an isolated incident, out of character for them both. 'Thank you for inviting me.'

His mouth twisted ironically. '*De nada.*' He was mocking her, aware of what she was trying to do and refusing to help or even permit it. 'You will come again.' It was a flat statement.

'I don't think so.' As she spoke Cass turned away so he

would not see what those words cost her. Sanity had returned and she was deeply disturbed by what had happened. It was not simply the kiss; she had been a willing partner. Rather it was the empathy, the intuitive recognition of like calling to like and the shutting out of the rest of the world that had her struggling fiercely with her conscience. *He was engaged to someone else.* One did not need to play with fire to know that it burned, and she had been tempted too close to a dangerous flame.

Gathering the reins, she swung up on to the mare's back, making unnecessary adjustments to one of the stirrup leathers in order to avoid looking at Miguel. For even the sight of him unsettled her, made her pulses race and her heart thud unevenly. And now, with the imprint of his lips still fresh on hers, she was having to fight a yearning she had never before experienced.

He brought the stallion alongside and they started back down the trail. 'I have to fly to Mexico City for the day,' Miguel announced after several minutes' silence, 'do you wish to come?'

His tone gave no clue to his own feelings, yet, Cass reasoned, he would not have mentioned it had he not been prepared for her to accept.

Without hesitating she replied, 'Thank you, but no. I prefer to spend today at the *hacienda*. The garden is very beautiful and the views are spectacular. I'll probably do some sketching, maybe start developing a few ideas for designs.'

'Very wise,' he agreed blandly. 'You have much to think about, do you not?' He leaned towards her, tall and perfectly relaxed in the saddle, his narrowed eyes glittering. 'Like a snail you have withdrawn into your shell, Cassandra. But you cannot hide from me.'

Her head snapped up. She was overwhelmed by sudden apprehension and the horribly familiar feeling of being pushed into a situation she didn't know how to handle. 'What do you want from me?' she cried.

The smile that lifted the corners of his mouth only emphasised the intensity in his eyes as they raked her from head to toe, returning to linger on her flushed face.

'Everything.'

The single word, uttered with flat finality, made Cass's heart skip a beat. The blood roared in her ears as she tried to grasp the full meaning of what he had said, but the task proved beyond her. Instead she seized on the only other explanation. It was a joke. He was teasing her and she, gullible as ever, had fallen for it.

Raking her scattered wits together, she flashed him a wry smile that trembled only slightly. 'But surely you already have everything? Wealth, position, a lovely house, a fascinating career that you enjoy, and,' Cass inwardly steeled herself, 'a beautiful fiancée.'

Miguel's reaction startled her. There was a sardonic note in the laughter that rebounded from the encircling hills. 'Indeed,' he agreed, expertly gentling the spirited stallion who had started at the sudden sound. 'I have all those things. And what more could any man ask for than a woman prepared to bow entirely to his wishes and pander to his every whim?' The clear note of cynicism puzzled Cass, but she had no time to think further as he went on, 'And what of you, Cassandra Elliott? Would you behave so for the man you loved?'

'No,' she said truthfully. She knew she could never totally submerge her own needs, her own personality, to please someone else, no matter how much she cared for them.

'I thought not.' She could not tell from his tone what he was thinking. 'But then, you would not love a man who could demand such a sacrifice.'

'No,' she admitted. 'Though to many women it might not seem a sacrifice. After all, to be lavishly clothed, fed, pampered and housed in return for one's undivided attention *appears* a fair exchange.'

One corner of his mouth tilted. 'What finesse!' he mocked. 'How gently you drive home the blade.' Cass's face flamed. 'However,' he continued, 'the relationship you descibe applies equally to loyal servants or even a trusted dog.'

Cass shrugged lightly. He had said it.

'You, on the other hand,' he taunted, 'are *quite* independent.'

Cass glanced uncertainly at him, sensing something unpleasant was coming, incapable of forestalling it.

'You live alone?' She nodded. 'Where?'

'I have a small flat not far from the company building.'

'You, like me, have a career you enjoy at which you are very successful.' He waited, clearly expecting confirmation, so she nodded again.

'Then what hold has Prentice got over you?' The question, put in cool, quiet tones, hit her like a slap.

She gasped. 'I don't know what you——'

He didn't let her finish. 'Do you think me stupid?' The demand was harsh with barely suppressed fury. '*You* tell me there is nothing between you, then *he* announces your engagement and you say nothing. I do not understand why you permit this unless you lied to me.'

'No,' Cass's voice was a strangled croak. 'No, I didn't. You don't underst——'

Miguel cut straight through her shocked denial. 'You are right. I don't understand. Prentice is using you and you are allowing it.' He glared at her, plainly finding it difficult to contain his disgust, a muscle jumping at the point of his jaw.

Her churning emotions vivid on her face, Cass tilted her chin to meet his eyes. 'Yes,' she said defiantly, 'I *have* been used. Misplaced loyalty is my only excuse.

That, and a reluctance to believe that a person I considered a colleague and friend could——' Her voice broke and she stopped, lowering her eyes and swallowing hard.

Blinking away sudden, scalding tears, she lifted her head to look at Miguel once more, her pain erupting like a lava flow and equally uncontainable. 'Derek is what he is. He drinks too much and no doubt that influences his behaviour.' Her chin lifted a fraction higher. 'But what's *your* excuse, Señor Ibarra?' She flung the words at him. 'How do you justify *your* hypocrisy?'

Miguel visibly paled then his proud features tightened to granite hardness. His eyes were flint. Lightning-fast he reached out and seized the mare's reins, bringing both horses to an abrupt halt. 'Explain.' The word was rapped out a terse, icy command.

'I should have thought it was obvious,' Cass flared back. 'Your opinion of me must be rock-bottom if you believe I would be a willing party to Derek's plans——'

'I didn't say you were willing,' he cut in coldly.

'No, you asked what *hold* he had over me. That implies blackmail, and to be blackmailed I'd have to have done something of which I was ashamed. So it amounts to the same thing, doesn't it,' Cass cried, 'my rotten character. Yet that didn't stop you *sampling the merchandise*,' she mocked bitterly, 'before turning on the righteous indignation.'

Unable to stop the tears that spilled down her hot cheeks, Cass snatched the reins back and with a reckless disregard for her own safety, or the steepness of the track, she slammed her heels into the mare's side.

With a squeal the animal leapt forward, her ears laid back, the whites of her eyes showing. Cass clung on as they hurtled in an avalanche of earth and stones down the lonely path. Her vision was blurred by tears and sobs of anger and humiliation wrenched her throat and chest.

'Cassandra!' Miguel's voice taut and urgent, echoed around her and she heard the stallion's hooves drumming as he gained on her.

She darted a glance over her shoulder. He was about ten yards behind and coming up fast.

'Leave me alone!' she cried.

His face mirrored anger and anxiety. 'All right, all right. Go on by yourself,' he shouted. 'But in God's name, slow down. If the mare breaks a leg I'll have to shoot her. Do you want that on your conscience?'

His words had the shocking effect of ice-water. Realising the enormity of what she had done, the danger in which her desperate flight had placed both herself and her mount, Cass pulled back on the reins. Tense, trembling with effort and reaction, she gripped the saddle with her thighs while the mare skidded and slid on the loose dirt and pebbles.

Miguel kept his word and remained some distance behind as they passed beneath the stand of oaks and approached the stable yard.

When Cass slid from the mare's back her legs shook so much she could barely stand. She rested her forehead against the animal's sweat-sheened neck as Miguel clattered into the yard.

Two grooms appeared from one of the store-rooms. She handed over the reins to one and the mare was led away to her stall. Cass turned to go and came face to face with Miguel.

Tightly controlled emotion had tautened the bronze skin across his high cheekbones. His eyes were splinters of ice that stopped her breath in her throat and made her take an involuntary step backwards.

'I'm sorry,' she whispered. 'I should not have put the mare at risk. She must be very valuable.'

'She is.' He was brusque. 'However, she is replaceable. You are not.'

Cass's eyes widened but before she could frame any sort of reply he said, 'Go on back to the house. They will all be down for breakfast soon. It is your decision whether or not to speak of our ride.' His tone was abrupt, impersonal. He gave the impression of not caring one way or the other.

But Cass knew without having to think about it that she would say nothing. Despite the way it had ended, and the raw pain and humiliation she had felt, watching the sun rise and listening to Miguel talk of his ancestors had been a profoundly moving experience. One too precious ever to share. He treasured the solitude and spiritual communion with the past that his morning ride provided in an otherwise busy and demanding life. She had been privileged to share it this once. Regardless of the way things stood between them now she would not abuse that privilege.

As he held her gaze, searching her eyes intently, she made a brief, negative movement with her head, and sensed quiet satisfaction in him.

Were his reasons for preferring silence on the matter the same as her own? Or was it simply more convenient that by remaining in ignorance Teresa and her parents would have no cause to question his motives for taking a woman other than his fiancée riding in the hills at dawn?

Weariness washed over her like a wave. What did it matter? She had given her word freely. She would keep it. Lowering her head, suddenly aware of her tear-stained cheeks and dishevelled appearance, she started past him. But one strong brown hand shot out to grip her wrist.

'There is much still to be said between us, Cassandra.' He spoke quietly.

Hurt flared again, a sharp stabbing. 'On the contrary,' she responded tightly, 'I think you said it all.'

His face darkened. 'I do not like women who sulk.'

Cass's head flew up, her eyes blazing at this brazen arrogance. *Sulk?* After the things he had said? The accusations he had made? 'And I can't stand men who patronise,' she retorted at once.

To her amazement and chagrin he began to laugh, a deep, full-throated laugh of genuine amusement. Angry, he was imposing, but laughter transformed him, adding a dimension to his devastating handsomeness that made Cass's heart lurch.

Raising her hand Miguel dropped a warm kiss on her palm, gazing at her from under his dark brows as a treacherous weakness assailed her. 'We will talk again, you and I,' he promised. Then with a mocking bow totally at odds with the intimacy of the moment before, he strode across the yard to speak to one of the grooms.

CHAPTER SEVEN

AFTER taking a shower, Cass had dressed once more in shirt, slacks and sweater. As well as washing off the dust and tear-stains, the hot water had soothed away her tormenting confusion, leaving a numbness that was oddly peaceful.

Adding a touch of colour to lips and eyelids, she brushed her hair to a coppery sheen and left it loose on her shoulders. Then, deliberately concentrating her thoughts on possible places to do her sketching, she went downstairs to breakfast.

Everyone else was already seated around the enormous table and Cass noticed immediately that they were all dressed for the city.

'You certainly slept well,' Derek said as she entered, his tone accusing.

'Yes, thank you,' she replied evenly, refusing to be drawn.

Miguel half rose from his chair. He too had showered. His black hair, curling thickly on his crisp shirt collar was still damp and his blunt jaw was freshly shaved. He wore his dark business suit with the same ease as his breeches and sweater, yet the air of distinction and authority it lent him was undeniable.

Cass shook her head, carefully avoiding his eyes, hoping the betraying heat in her cheeks was less visible than it felt. 'Please don't get up. I'll help myself.' She went to the sideboard.

The physical exertion of the ride, the crisp fresh air and the emotional upheaval of the morning had combined, much to her own surprise, to make her hungry. Helping herself to eggs, tortillas and sweet rolls, she carried the plates to the table and slid quietly into the only vacant chair. This time she was between Derek and Señor Morelos, directly opposite Miguel.

'I knocked on your door a couple of times,' Derek went on, staring hard at her, 'but you never answered.'

'I expect I was in the shower,' Cass replied lightly and reached for the coffee-pot.

'What, for half an hour?'

Realising Derek was in one of his argumentative moods, and determined there would not be *another* scene, Cass turned to face him. 'Was there some important reason you wanted to speak to me so early?'

Taken aback by her unexpected directness, Derek fumbled for words, 'Well, no, not exactly. But——'

'Then it really doesn't matter, does it,' she interrupted pleasantly and Derek's mouth thinned to a hard, white line.

Having fetched another sweet roll from the sideboard, Teresa lowered herself with studied elegance into her chair and leaned towards Miguel, pouting provocatively. 'And you, no doubt, were out on your beloved Diablo.'

'What's a Diablo?' Derek demanded, but before Miguel could reply, waved him to silence with a careless gesture. Closing his eyes and making a visible show of thinking hard with one hand pressed to his forehead, Derek announced, 'No, hang on, it's one of those new racing bikes, isn't it?' His eyes flew open and he sat back in his chair, a self-satisfied smirk twisting his mouth. 'I think one won some trophy or other at Silverstone a couple of weeks back. Mind you, *I* don't think they're up to much, all show and little substance if you ask me. Still, if you're happy with it ...' He shrugged.

Miguel remained silent for several seconds and only by the whiteness around his nostrils and the imperceptible deepening of the creases on either side of his mouth was Cass aware of the deep displeasure Derek's manner was causing him.

'I know nothing of this machine,' he said at last. 'My Diablo is just a horse.'

A dull flush spread over Derek's face.

'For shame, Miguel,' Teresa scolded. 'Just a horse indeed!' She turned to Derek. 'Diablo is a very valuable stallion.' Her kohl-darkened eyes sparkled. 'He is worth many thousands of dollars. Lots of people want to buy him. Miguel could ask any sum he wanted, but he will not sell.'

Cass stole a quick glance at Teresa. The girl had not mentioned the stallion's beauty, spirit or intelligence. Had she not noticed the satin gloss of his coat? The harnessed power in his flowing movement? Did she see everything only in terms of its monetary value?

Cass let her glance linger. Despite the relatively early hour Teresa looked as though an army of beauticians had been at work on her. Her gleaming hair was swept up into an elegant French pleat and her lavish make-up was flawless. She was wearing a pencil-slim black skirt with a split up the side to just above her knee, emphasising her shapely nyloned legs; hand-made court shoes in black patent leather, and a batwing-sleeved sweater of fine mohair, boldly patterned in cyclamen and black.

Turning her attention to Miguel, Teresa rested her chin on one smooth white hand and Cass noticed that her nail varnish had been changed to match her sweater. Gazing at the tall, dark man beside her, Teresa demanded petulantly, 'Why don't you ever take me on your dawn rides?'

Miguel gave her an indulgent smile. 'Because you and I both know that the sun would have been up an hour before you had even decided what to wear.'

Despite her determination not to dwell on matters she was painfully aware were none of her business, Cass could not avoid noticing that Miguel's attitude towards Teresa resembled that of an elder brother. There was nothing of the ardent lover in either his speech or the looks he directed at the raven-haired girl. Yet they *were* betrothed, and Cass knew enough about Mexican customs to realise that such an arrangement was not entered into lightly, nor was it easily broken.

So what of this morning? What of those things he had told her, things she sensed he spoke of rarely, if at all. He had said he wanted *everything* from her. What had he meant? What could she ever be in these circumstances?

Knowing she had no right to condemn him for the treachery of her own heart only increased the helpless misery welling up in her.

Teresa tossed her head angrily. 'That is not fair, Miguel. Look at the time. It is barely nine o'clock. Am I not ready for the day?'

'Indeed,' he agreed smoothly, 'and you look ...' he paused fractionally, 'wonderful. But I was saddling Diablo three hours ago. Where were you then?'

Cass's stomach muscles tightened as she wondered where the conversation would lead.

Then their eyes met. His gaze was smoke-dark, gleaming with silent laughter and something else, something that sent a flood of warmth tingling through her. Her heart thudded unevenly and her mouth grew dry. She looked away quickly, shaken, unwilling to believe he would take such a risk, yet unable to deny what she knew to be true.

Quite deliberately, and in front of all his guests, though they were unaware of it, he was reminding her of what had occurred between them, and of his promise that things were by no means settled.

Salvation came from an unlikely source.

'Enough, Teresa,' her father said gruffly. 'Miguel and I have a busy day ahead of us. A man needs peace to gather his thoughts and decide his course of action. If Miguel finds tranquillity riding like the *charros*, you must respect his wishes and let him be.'

'Miguel is not a cowboy,' Teresa objected hotly, interpreting her father's remark as insulting.

'Oh, but I was once,' Miguel corrected her. 'I rode with the men, ate the same food, looked after my own horse and took orders from the foreman.'

'That was years ago,' Teresa said impatiently. 'You were only a boy. Now you are an important and wealthy businessman.'

'And as such I should forget my past?' Beneath Miguel's quiet enquiry was an irony that brought Cass's head up in a swift, startled movement. Her eyes met Miguel's in an instant of total accord.

Aware of Derek's moody gaze on her, she began to fold her napkin, recognising another truth. Teresa was a snob, and wanted no reminders of anything Miguel had done before reaching his present position. Did her reluctance to accept all that had made him the man he now was extend to his more distant past? His Aztec blood?

Cass had her answer as Teresa shrugged her shoulders impatiently.

'Well, none of it is relevant any more. It is not healthy always to be looking back,' she stated. 'Do you not agree, Derek?'

Derek hesitated, clearly torn between ingratiating himself with Teresa and further antagonising Miguel.

'If a man has a fiancée as beautiful as you,' he managed at last with heavy gallantry, 'I cannot imagine why he would ever wish to look at *anything* else.'

Teresa laughed delightedly and caressed Derek's arm, her long, perfectly painted nails grazing the back of his hand in a deliberately provocative gesture. 'You must accompany us today,' she decided. 'Miguel is taking us in the helicopter to Mexico City. Papa is fighting a take-over bid for our textile mills so he and Miguel have meetings all day. But Mama and I are going shopping. You and Cass could see some of the city and meet us for lunch.'

'Wonderful!' Derek agreed with enthusiasm, then turned to Cass. 'It won't take you long to change, will it?'

Cass pushed her empty plate carefully to one side. 'I'm sure you'll have a marvellous time.'

'Of course we will,' Derek nodded, then his smile faded. 'What d'you mean? You're coming as well.'

'No, I'd rather stay here and do some sketching.' Cass was quiet but firm.

Derek looked furious and was about to argue but Teresa forestalled him.

'I'm sure the rest will do you good, though of course we shall miss you.' Her smile was dazzling and totally insincere. 'You do look tired, and so thin. Maybe you should forget this work of yours and spend a few days in bed to recover your strength.'

Bitch, Cass thought with uncharacteristic vehemence. The back of her neck prickled with a mixture of anger and amusement. 'Thank you for your concern,' she said sweetly, 'but I am perfectly well. However, as I explained, this is a working holiday for me and I intend to make a start while the ideas are still fresh in my mind.'

Teresa's delicate shrug indicated that, as far as she was concerned, the matter was closed.

But Derek was a different proposition.

'I didn't invite you to come in,' Cass pointed out when he threw open the door to her room a few minutes later. The calmness of her tone was belied by the immediate tension knotting her stomach.

Ignoring her remark he went straight into action. 'Why won't you come?'

Cass finished repairing her lipstick with a hand that had grown faintly unsteady, and began putting her make-up away. 'I told you, I have my own plans.'

Derek clenched his fists. 'I'm not putting up with this. We're *engaged*, for God's sake, You've *got* to come.'

Cass turned to face him. 'You're mistaken,' she said coldly. 'I haven't *got* to do anything.'

'You're going back on your word.' He was deliberately working himself up into a frenzy of righteous indignation. 'You're trying to make me look a fool.'

'If you look a fool Derek, that's entirely your own doing,' Cass snapped, 'and as for my word, I never gave it. You made all the announcements without consulting me at all. Then you tried to pressure me into going along with each devious new scheme. Well, forget it, Derek. I am *not* going to marry you. I never had any intention of doing so.' She walked over to the window and pushed the curtains further back, trying to stifle the upsurge of anger. She turned to him once more. 'It's as much my fault as yours. I should have told you sooner, made it absolutely clear from the moment we arrived and you told Miguel that we were unofficially engaged.'

'Why didn't you then?' he snarled. 'Why let me go on thinking—hoping——'

Cass hung on to her temper. 'Because I didn't want to embarrass you in front of everyone else. I was trying to spare your feelings.' There was an edge of bitterness to her wry laugh. 'You didn't give a thought to mine though, did you? I was under the plainly ridiculous impression that we were friends. But since we got on that plane to come out here, it's been all too obvious that you and I have entirely different concepts of friendship.'

A variety of expressions had crossed Derek's face while she was speaking. There was a brief silence while she watched him visibly struggling to come to terms with what she had said.

He sank down on the edge of the bed, spreading his hands, palms up, in a gesture of utter helplessness. Then, to her horrified amazement, tears gathered in his pale eyes and rolled down his cheeks to drip from his freshly shaved chin.

'Cass, I'm sorry,' he whispered huskily, and leaning forward, elbows resting on his widespread knees, his hands hanging loosely between them, he lowered his head. 'I've been a complete bastard.'

She stared at him, unable to move, her thoughts racing, doubt uppermost in her mind.

'You've never understood what it's like for me,' he muttered, staring at the beige carpet. 'The only son being groomed to take over the family business. So much expected yet so many bloody constrictions. I got a degree in Economics and a diploma in Business Studies. But whenever I try to put what I've learned into practice, I run into walls at every turn.' He made a face and mimicked, 'This is the way it's always been; that is how we've always done it; it's always worked before so why change now; new is not necessarily right, nor is forward always progress!' His voice reverted to normal, tinged with disgust. 'I've heard them all, every reason and excuse for *not* doing anything. But when I wanted out, the roof fell in. How could I even *think* of leaving? This was my legacy, my responsibility, the whole purpose of my life.' He broke off, shaking his head despairingly.

Cass was appalled as she realised the kind of pressure he must have been under. She began to feel guilty.

'I'm not the world's strongest character, Cass.' He gazed up at her, his eyes full of suffering, his cheeks wet. 'I've never pretended to be. When it all got too much and the frustration was unbearable, I took a drink or two, or three. It was the only way I could cope. It took the edge off a bit. I thought you understood. You used to.' There was a note of complaint in his voice.

Cass recalled the countless times she had forgiven him, glossed over his drunken behaviour and its resulting embarrassment and unpleasantness.

Doubt reared its head again. He had always blamed *her* for his drinking. He had claimed it was due to frustration over her refusal to sleep with him. Never before had he ever mentioned other pressures. In fact, he had usually appeared to get the better of his father in their business discussions, steam-rollering his way over Matthew Prentice's quietly voiced objections.

It dawned on her that he was doing what he had always done, playing on her sympathy and good nature, quite clearly expecting her once again to forgive and forget.

At last she saw him for what he was, and this new lucidity, springing as it did from the changes in herself, dissolved her anger into pity.

'It's no good, Derek,' she said softly, sadly. 'It's not going to work.' Seeing his expression harden and his mouth compress into a thin line, she stopped. She had made her point. It would be unkind to rub salt in the wound.

He sat up and took a handkerchief from his trouser pocket. Cass looked tactfully away as he wiped his eyes.

His snort of laughter startled her.

'Oh well,' he said blithely, as he stood up, rubbing his hands together, 'it was worth a try. You've always swallowed my abject apologies before.'

She gazed at him, wide-eyed. He *couldn't* mean that the way it sounded, that it had all been an act. He had let his guard down, revealing some of the pressures that drove him. He must be trying, all too clumsily, to cover his embarrassment. His next words proved her totally wrong.

'I thought the tears were an inspired touch, quite heart-rending really.' He sounded as objective as a critic reviewing a play. 'I was sure they'd get to you.' The only emotion in his voice was injured pride.

Cass was incapable of speech.

'The problem is,' Derek continued, talking as much to himself as her, 'what do we do now? You see, I'm not prepared to accept that our engagement is broken.'

Exasperation freed Cass's tongue. 'There *was* no engagement,' she exploded.

'Don't be silly.' Tone and expression held the pained irritation of a parent to a recalcitrant child. 'You didn't contradict me when I told Ibarra as we were getting into the helicopter, or when I made the announcement last night.'

'I explained all that,' Cass protested.

'Oh yes. You were waiting for the right moment.' Sarcasm twisted his mouth. 'However, that's beside the point.'

'Just what *is* the point?' Cass demanded, desperately trying to regain some control of the situation, infuriated by a flutter of fear she could not entirely ignore.

'Come on,' he sneered. 'You and that imperious so and so. Don't bother to deny it.' He held up his hands as she opened her mouth to protest. 'If you are determined to make our little disagreement public, there are one or two matters I shall have to bring to our host's attention.'

'Such as?' Cass's throat was paper-dry.

'Such as you destroying the letters Jorge Ibarra sent asking us to postpone our visit for three months.'

'But why should I do that?' Cass challenged him.

'So that Miguel would be forced by the laws of hospitality to put us up and you could use your——' he ran his eyes lewdly down her body, '——charm to get our company a special deal.'

Cass gritted her teeth. The first part at least was so

plausible. Miguel *had* said he was obliged to follow his father's wishes and put them up. And there had been open doubt in his eyes when she had said she never received his father's letter. 'But I didn't even know Miguel existed until he met us at the airport,' she cried.

'Do you think *he'll* believe that when I've finished?'

Suddenly Cass stiffened. 'Three months, you said. How did you know Jorge Ibarra wanted our visit postponed for *three months*?' She gasped. '*You* destroyed those letters.'

'God, you're quick,' he sneered.

Cass was stunned. It shook her deeply to hear him admit it. A thought struck her. 'Derek, about the alarm——'

His eyes narrowed and his expression was suddenly guarded. 'That was an accident.' He must have recognised the doubt on her face. 'You'll never prove anything,' he blustered. 'Ibarra can count those stones till he's black in the face. There are none missing.'

'Why, Derek?' Cass was utterly bewildered. 'Why are you doing this?'

His expression grew pinched and tight. 'I've got him over a barrel and he knows it.'

'I don't understand.' Cass shook her head violently. 'What are you talking about?'

Derek thrust his hand into his pockets, hunching his shoulders. 'You.'

Cass tensed. 'What about me?'

He began to pace up and down the room. 'Before we came here things were going along pretty well. You were getting more—friendly. I figured a holiday, preferably somewhere exotic, would loosen you up a bit. Let me past the "keep off" signs. That's why I fixed to come with you on this trip. You've given me a hard time, Cass. I've put up with more and hung about longer for you than any other woman. You've really had me going with his "hands off, don't touch" routine.'

Cass bit her tongue hard. If she interrupted him now she might never get to the bottom of it.

'Then Jorge's letter arrived. As soon as I'd read mine, got yours off your desk before you came in, and burned them both. I wasn't having anything mess up all my plans. I know I shouldn't have drunk so much on the plane, but I was nervous. I'd waited and planned so long and I was nearly home and dry.'

Cass could hardly believe her ears. Had she, even without meaning to, given him any encouragement to believe she felt that way about him? Her certainty reasserted itself. No, she had not. He had spun his own fantasy and such was his self-centredness that without any thought for her he had contrived to turn it into reality.

'But the moment Ibarra arrived in his bloody helicopter and walked into the airport building, so damned proud and arrogant, I sensed trouble. And I was right.' He stopped pacing and faced her, his mouth twisted in a bitter smile. 'So I decided I'd make you both pay, one way or another.'

Teresa's voice floated up the stairs. 'Derek, you must come now. We're leaving.'

He opened the door and called, 'I'll be right with you,' then turned back to Cass, his grin as cold and humourless as a shark's. 'Why hasn't he thrown me out? I've deliberately needled him, yet not once has he reacted with anything but that damned, high-and-mighty courtesy. He's put up with stuff from me he'd have killed anyone else for. Why, Cass? I'll tell you. Because if I go, you have to go. After all, he's engaged, isn't he, and it wouldn't do in this country to have a young, attractive, unattached woman staying in his house alone. So to keep you here he'll put up with anything I dish out.'

'Th-that's ridiculous!' Cass stammered.

Derek continued as though she hadn't spoken. 'Just remember, he might fancy you, and he'll take all he can persuade you to give, but you're nothing more than a diversion, an appetiser before the main course.'

Teresa called again, volubly impatient.

'Coming,' Derek shouted and smirked at Cass over his shoulder. 'And what a succulent dish that is. She's a lot more friendly than some I could mention.'

'Derek, you can't,' Cass was horrified.

'Why not?' he countered. 'Teresa isn't objecting. I've a suspicion she's one neglected girl and not too happy about it. Of course, if you were to start behaving like a fiancée, I wouldn't need to look elsewhere. So,' he shrugged, 'it's all up to you, isn't it?'

With difficulty, Cass kept all expression out of her voice. 'That's blackmail.'

He flushed briefly. 'Just a little friendly persuasion.'

She stared at him for a long moment, fighting the nausea that burned in her throat. She had to swallow hard before she could speak. 'There is not and never has been any engagement between us, Derek. If you don't tell them, I will.'

The smug satisfaction that had begun to settle on his features as the silence grew melted away, replaced by disbelief. 'Do you realise what you're *doing?*' His voice cracked.

She didn't reply. She knew only too well what she was doing. What she did not know and could not guess was how far *he* would go in his lust for revenge. She didn't have to wait long to find out.

His pale eyes seemed suddenly bloodshot, as though his fury was too much to contain. 'You'll regret this,' he hissed.

Still Cass said nothing, aware as never before of being entirely alone in a strange place with no one to turn to

'I'll seduce Teresa,' he threatened. 'Ibarra will be a laughing stock, and I'll make sure he blames you.'

'I am not responsible for Teresa.' Cass forced the words out past sudden, gut-wrenching fear. What *had* she done? Yet how could she have acted differently and retained any shred of integrity?

His eyes glittering with malice and wounded pride, Derek fired his parting shot. 'As of this moment, you're fired.' He glared at her in savage triumph, waiting, daring her to protest.

They both knew he did not have the power to dismiss her without referring to the other directors. But he could make her working life so difficult and unpleasant if she chose to defy him and stay that, even as the possibility occurred, she discarded it.

'As you like,' she said calmly, managing to hide her shock at this added blow. Yet she should have expected it. No matter what happened now, or to what extent he blackened her character, she knew she had made the only possible choice.

The door slammed, making her jump. He had gone. She heard him hurrying down the stairs, calling out apologies with such charm and sincerity she could almost believe he meant them. She shook her head and drew in a deep, slightly tremulous breath. Now all she could do was wait. It would be a *long* day.

A momentary dread turned her legs to water and she reached out to the window frame for support. What if Miguel believed the things Derek told him about her?

She would know when next she saw him, in that first instant, before he even spoke.

The helicopter swished overhead with a clattering roar and Cass watched it disappear over the hills. Until Miguel returned she had to keep her mind occupied or she would go mad. For no matter how hard she tried to convince herself otherwise, his opinion of her mattered more than anything else in the world.

Collecting her sketch-pad and pencil, she went downstairs and out of the house. Climbing the paddock fence, she perched on the top bar and surveyed the panorama spread below her.

Maybe losing her job wasn't such a bad thing. She had worked more or less independently anyway. Perhaps she would go freelance. Set up her own workshop and sell direct to the public. Or would it be better to use an agent? She had some money put by so she didn't have to rush into anything, and her name was well known. She would think of it not as a disaster, but an opportunity.

She began to work, her pencil flying over the thick pad, capturing in bold strokes the rolling vista of dry hills, the arching sky, stunted trees and spiky cacti. She filled page after page, varying her subjects, and spent over an hour on several studies of marigolds, Mexico's favourite flower.

The sun climbed higher. Consuelo called her for a light lunch and afterwards, instead of taking a siesta, Cass sat in the cool shade of the oaks and recreated on paper the glory of the sunrise she had experienced that morning.

A sudden heavy shower drove her to the stables for shelter. She sought out the mare's stall and after obtaining, through a mixture of sign language and broken Spanish, the groom's agreement, she spent some time brushing the satiny coat, talking softly to the animal, trying to make amends for the morning's headlong dash.

Later, she went out again and walked up the hill that looked down on the *hacienda*. There she stayed, each stroke of her pencil engraving the scene on her heart, until the fading light and cooling air drove her up to her room to shower and change for dinner.

Once back in the house tension formed a knot in her stomach that began to twist and turn. The hours alone and the deep satisfaction she always obtained from her preliminary sketching, knowing she was laying the foundations for new, exciting designs, had given her some much-needed peace. But they would all be back soon. What would happen then?

As her imagination threw up one horrific scene after another, her appetite disappeared and she grew more and more nervous.

She could of course stay in her room, but that would be tantamount to an admission of guilt or shame. She had no regrets about the stand she had made. But did she have the courage to sit through dinner under the condemning gaze of five pairs of eyes? For condemn they would, Derek would see to that.

Maybe they would all ignore her, simply pretend she didn't exist. No, Miguel would not permit it. Whatever his private thoughts, she was a guest in his father's house and as such would receive his courtesy.

Miguel. Cass pressed cold hands to her flushed cheeks. He was beginning to matter far too much, and that road could only lead to heartbreak. Common sense counselled distance, both physical and emotional. Yet even Derek, for all his self-absorption, had noticed the magnetic pull that drew Miguel and herself into each other's orbit. And when he touched her—she wrenched her thoughts away. This was pointless. Worse, it was self-destructive. She was free, he was not. That was all there was to it. No matter how *she* felt, and she wasn't sure exactly what she did feel, she could be nothing more to him than a passing attraction. Somehow she had to scrape up enough willpower, pride and dignity to keep him at arm's length.

Of course, if he accepted and believed Derek's version of events, the problem would no longer exist, for there would be no teasing warmth in his eyes, no challenging light, only icy disgust.

How would she bear it? Her head swam and she sank down on the bed, hugging her arms across her body. The soft velour robe provided neither warmth nor comfort as she shivered uncontrollably.

There was a light tap on the door. Before Cass could answer it opened and Consuelo put her head in. '*Señorita*, is phone call for you.'

Cass stared blankly at the housekeeper. 'For me?'

'*Sí, señorita*. Is Don Miguel. He call from Mexico City. Is very bad line.'

Cass's heart gave a wild leap and hammered against her ribs. Not daring to imagine what it might mean, she ran bare-footed down the stairs.

After taking a deep breath that did nothing to stop the tremor in her hands or the deafening thunder of her heartbeat, she lifted the receiver from the mosaic table. 'H-hello?'

'Cassandra? We will not be back tonight.' It was impossible to discern any expression in the disembodied voice.

She swallowed. 'I see. Thank you for letting me know.' She was gripping the phone so tightly her hand was wet and slippery with perspiration and her knuckles ached. Why were they staying over? Was it for a celebration? Or to spare everyone further embarrassment? Was it because of her? *She had to know.* 'Are the meetings running late?' Even to her own ears the desperate casualness rang horribly false.

'. . . finished for the moment.' His words were almost drowned by a loud crackling. '. . . not . . . worry . . . been . . . accident . . . calling . . . hospital . . .' More crackling cut him off.

'Miguel!' she shouted, her voice hoarse with strain.

'Are you still there? Miguel?' What had happened? Who had been hurt?

'... row morning,' was all she heard, then the line went dead.

CHAPTER EIGHT

As SHE toyed with the delicious meal Consuelo had prepared for her, Cass forced herself to think logically. Whatever had happened, it couldn't be *that* serious if they were all coming back in the morning. And as it was Miguel who had phoned, he couldn't be badly hurt. In fact, he might not have been involved at all.

She caught herself, realising the significance of her thoughts. He was was the only one who mattered. *She had to stop this.*

After a restless night punctuated with dreams she could not remember, but which had filled her with a deep sense of unease, she eventually fell into an exhausted sleep, only to be woken three hours later by Consuelo bringing in her breakfast. She forced the food down then stumbled, heavy eyed, into the shower.

Dressed in a cinnamon blouse, her Aran jacket and cream pants tucked into her tan leather boots, she was trying to disguise her pallor and the violet shadows beneath her eyes, when she heard the helicopter approaching. Leaving her hair loose and her make-up scattered all over the top of the chest of drawers, she flew downstairs and out on to the drive as the helicopter touched down gently between the paddock and the house.

Teresa was the first one out, her mink-lined raincoat bundled under her arm. She was followed by her parents. Cass's anxious eyes could detect no sign of anything wrong with any of them as Teresa's high heels crunched importantly across the fine gravel. That could only mean one thing.

'What happened?' Cass started forward.

'After what you did, you need to ask?' Teresa delivered the words with a scathing glare and swished past in a cloud of expensive perfume.

Nodding politely to Señor and Señora Morelos, who stared stonily ahead as they passed her, Cass hurried towards the helicopter.

Her heart soared as she saw that Miguel had climbed out of the pilot's seat and was leaning into the cabin. It immediately plummeted as she realised the casualty had to be Derek and, judging by Teresa's reaction, the blame had been laid very firmly on her shoulders. But Miguel was safe. He had flown them back. She touched his arm, relief and pleasure at seeing him again overpowering all her intentions to retain a barrier between them. 'Can I help?'

He swung round and she gasped, 'Oh, no,' her eyes widening in shock at the purple swelling on his temple bisected by four neat stitches holding the edges of an inch-long cut together.

For an instant his eyes softened and he looked pleased to see her, but the impression was fleeting for within a heartbeat his features had set in a cold mask. 'Don't worry, I'll live.' The deep voice was tired and the sardonic tone did not quite hide an undercurrent of anger. His eyes, meeting hers for a moment, were narrowed with strain, and Cass guessed he had a blinding headache. 'Which is more than will be said for him if he doesn't pull himself together.' His distaste was plain as he reached in to finish unbuckling Derek's seat-belt.

Cass caught a brief glimpse of Derek's face, paper-white and sheened with perspiration, before he slumped forward into Miguel's arms. 'Is he hurt?' she whispered.

'Not as much as he deserves to be,' came the grim reply.

'What happened?' Cass asked.

As Miguel heaved the barely conscious Derek out on to the drive, her nose wrinkled at the smell of stale alcohol, stronger than the pungent antiseptic.

'Close the door, will you?' Miguel said over his shoulder. She slammed it shut and hurried to take Derek's other arm and relieve Miguel of some of the load.

'You mean you don't know what's behind all this?' Miguel threw a cynical glance across at her as they dragged Derek up the steps, into the hall and towards the stairs. 'Haven't you used him shamefully? Misled him into believing you loved him and intended to marry him, only to throw him over when a better prospect appeared on the horizon?'

Cass went cold then hot all over. Her face burned and dismay and rage boiled up in her. Although he had threatened, she had not been able to convince herself that Derek would actually go through with it. It had clearly taken a lot of alcohol to boost his courage. For a split second she longed to throw off the weight of Derek's arm and slap his face with all her strength.

But Miguel was talking again, his voice calm, level and quite expressionless. 'Apparently, he poured all this out to Teresa and her mother over lunch. Then, not wishing to burden them further with his troubles he said he would spend the afternoon sight-seeing alone.'

'In the nearest bar, no doubt,' Cass muttered, ashamed, hurt and furious all at once.

'He came to the bank where Don Diego and I were attending a meeting.' Cass felt a chasm opening up beneath her feet. 'The staff could see he had been drinking and tried to pacify him, but he broke into our conference. It seems he has somehow conceived the idea that I am responsible for your change of heart towards him.'

Cass closed her eyes briefly and kept her head down as they manoeuvred Derek through the door and across the room on to his bed.

Consuelo appeared in the doorway and addressed Miguel in a flood of Spanish, tutting and shaking her head. Teresa pushed into the group.

'Miguel, I will attend to this.' Without waiting for his assent she turned to the housekeeper. 'Fetch Juan or Tomás from the stables to undress Señor Prentice and help him to bed. The hospital said he must rest for twenty-four hours in case of the concussion.'

Consuelo raised her eyebrows in silent query as she looked to Miguel and when he nodded, she shrugged and left.

'This need not affect our arrangements for the weekend,' Teresa announced briskly. 'Derek should have recovered tomorrow and we can fly down in the afternoon as planned. Perhaps the festivities will help him forget his unhappiness.' She shot a venomous glare at Cass, who flinched. 'I think, Miss Elliott, you should leave now——'

'Teresa!' The word left Miguel's lips like a pistol shot, and she stopped abruptly, switching her gaze to him. He continued in quiet warning, 'Do not presume too much.'

Her dark eyes widened. '*Querido*,' her tone was stricken, 'I only want to help. You have so much on your mind.' She came towards him, laying one slim hand on his lapel, smoothing the expensive material. 'I know Papa values your advice concerning the takeover. There is also the estate to run as well as the business, and your own father must be much on your mind. Unexpected guests at this time have only added to these worries.' She pouted up at him. 'What kind of fiancée would I be if I could not at least take the running of the household from your shoulders?'

Watching his face out of the corner of her eye, Cass
saw it assume the expression of wry amusement
underlaid with cynicism he habitually wore when
talking to Teresa. It piqued her curiosity like a snagging
thorn.

'Your concern for my responsibilities does you great
credit, Teresa.' Miguel plucked her hand from his lapel
and after touching it lightly to his lips, released it.

At that moment, Tomás, the groom from whom Cass
had obtained permission to visit the mare, entered the
room, somewhat reluctantly, in front of the housekeeper. As Miguel gave him instructions in Spanish,
Cass found herself puzzling over Miguel's words to
Teresa. Then it dawned. It was not concern for *him*
that prompted Teresa's display of organisational ability.
In any case, her concern seemed more for Derek than
Miguel. Teresa, anticipating her future role as mistress
of the *hacienda*, wanted to use this opportunity to
establish herself as such. But Miguel was warning her
off. *Why?*'

With a gesture that brooked no argument, Miguel
ushered Teresa, the housekeeper and Cass herself, out of
the room and closed the door. 'Consuelo, please take
coffee to the sitting-room for Señor and Señora
Morelos.'

'I will have mine in my room, Consuelo.' Teresa
announced haughtily. 'I have a million things to do
before we leave for San Miguel.' She swept a frosty gaze
over Cass before turning once more to Miguel. 'You
have no objection if I check on Derek's progress now and
then? It is not right that he is left entirely alone but I do
not think he would wish any visitors.' She flashed Cass a
barbed glance that was full of accusation.

'You do not need my permission if you wish to play
the nurse,' Miguel said coolly and again Cass was aware
of the strange undercurrent. How could Teresa not be

aware of it? Or was she simply choosing to ignore what she did not wish to hear?

Miguel glanced at his watch as Teresa stalked off down the passage. Cass, painfully aware that she was out of place, backed away. 'If you'll excuse me,' she mumbled. 'I'll——' She got no further.

Miguel's hand shot out, his strong fingers closing around her upper arm. 'You come with me,' he announced, hustling her towards the stairs.

'What for? Where to?' Her heart was hammering and her knees felt weak. There was an implacable determination about him.

'To my study. I want to talk to you without any interruptions.' With easy strength he half dragged, half pushed her across the hall and through the heavy oak door, closing it firmly behind him.

Once inside, he let go of her arm and raked both hands through his hair. It was a gesture of weariness that tugged at Cass's heart even as she rubbed the place where his fingers had closed with bruising strength on her arm.

Afraid he might see the feelings she was unable to hide, she turned from him and, taking a couple of steps away, traced with restless fingers the gold embossing on the edge of the heavy leather-topped desk. Its entire surface was piled with books, invoices, letters, circulars and other paperwork relating to a large, productive estate. Though clearly a masculine environment, the spacious room was comfortably furnished with leather armchairs on either side of a stone fireplace. An antique bookcase with glass doors stood against one wall. On the opposite wall, leather-bound ledgers were stacked on modern shelves. Two grey metal filing cabinets stood beside long windows that opened out on to the flower-decked veranda, and Indian rugs were scattered over the polished wood floor.

Cass wrenched her attention back to the problems facing her. There was only one course of action she could take. Clasping her hands tightly together, her nails digging into her flesh, she turned towards him.

'I——' Her voice faltered and she had to start again. 'I can't tell you how much I regret what has happened.' Her voice sounded as though it belonged to someone else. Her eyes were drawn to the ugly wound on his temple. He would carry the scar for life. The pain in her chest was like a knife. 'I will pack my things and leave today. I can go to an hotel in Queretaro.' Her voice faltered again. 'I should have done that as soon as I realised your father was not here and that you did not expect me—us.'

He gazed intently at her for several moments and she sensed he was weighing something in his mind.

'Regardless of what Derek may have told you,' she added quietly, 'I did not receive your father's letter. Had I done so, I would not have come. It was not for a business deal that I planned to visit Mexico. I was coming on holiday. Yes, I intended to gather ideas and materials for new designs, but there was no urgency about it.' She broke off.

'No,' he said abruptly. 'You will not leave. I will not permit it.'

She raised startled eyes to his. 'Why not? We have caused you nothing but trouble since we arrived.'

'The other things Prentice said, is there truth in them?' Miguel rapped out the question with the cold incisiveness of an interrogator. His features were stone-hard and his eyes burned like black coals beneath his heavy brows.

Cass flinched. 'What does that matter—if you believe him.'

'I want to hear from you,' he grated. 'Answer me, Cassandra.'

'Wh-what are you going to do about Derek?' she stammered.

He shrugged lightly. 'I have not yet decided. But why should you concern yourself?' He studied her intently.

'I—I'm not. It's just——'

'Aaaah,' he broke in, comprehension lifting one corner of his mouth in a surprisingly gentle smile. 'You fear for your job perhaps, if Prentice thinks we have discussed all this? Do not worry. I give you my word. Nothing that has happened here will make trouble in your work.'

Cass's lashes fluttered down to hide her quick dismay. 'Th-thank you,' she managed. He did not know Derek had sacked her and she could not tell him. That would place him in a position of feeling responsible for her, and she had been, albeit unwittingly, the cause of enough problems and embarrassment for him.

'Now, answer my question.'

Her mind still whirling, she glanced up at him, nonplussed.

'Prentice's accusations.' A hard undertone threaded his barely controlled impatience.

Her face flaming, she looked him straight in the eye. 'I have never at any time given Derek reason to believe he was anything more than a friend and colleague.' She moistened her lips which were paper-dry. He had to believe her. He *had* to. 'The engagement announcement was made without my knowledge or consent, and any hints or insinuations that he and I were or are ... close ... in any way are figments of his imagination.'

'Why did you not tell me this before?' he demanded.

Cass shrugged helplessly. 'I did try, once. But it was a private matter. Something I had to sort out and put a stop to myself. It would have been quite wrong to involve you.'

He raised one hand to the swollen gash on his temple,

his mouth twisting in a wry smile. 'Oh, I think I'm involved.'

Cass flushed even more deeply, her eyes falling away from his. She hugged her arms across her body. 'Please—how did it happen?' The words came out with a jerk.

'He threw a marble inkstand at me,' Miguel replied evenly. 'An impressive aim for one so—upset.'

Cass gulped. 'A-and the m-meeting?'

'Adjourned until later today,' came the succinct reply. 'You must admit that discussion of legal technicalities in business funding would have been something of an anti-climax after such an outburst.'

'But how ... I mean ... Derek—what did you do?'

Miguel raked his black hair once more and pushed one hand into his trouser pocket. 'I? Nothing. But my colleagues did not think it advisable for him to leave. In restraining him they were a little—shall we say— forceful? Apparently—I did not see it, being somewhat preoccupied—as he was persuaded to lie down, he hit his head on the corner of the boardroom table. He is fortunate to have such a thick skull.'

Cass shivered and had to bite her lip to restrain the hysterical laughter that bubbled inside her.

Miguel had recounted the event without any visible emotion yet Cass could imagine only too clearly the horrifying reality; Derek ranting and raving, struggling wildly as Miguel's shocked colleagues tried to prevent further violence; Miguel lying dazed and bloody, his reputation called into question; and the inevitable question leaping into the mind of every lawyer, financier and business executive present—*was it true?*

As her hands flew to her mouth, he went on calmly, 'Don Ricardo and Señor Castellas wanted to call the police, but I dissuaded them. It was galling enough to admit the man was a guest in my house and therefore, in theory at least, under my protection. However, even they conceded that takeovers attract enough problems without adding unnecessary complications.'

'What did you do?' Cass croaked.

'Don Ricardo's Mercedes has tinted windows, so he took Prentice and me to the hospital. Don Diego went to meet his wife and Teresa and they returned to their villa for the night. Prentice was kept in overnight for observation.'

'And what about you?' Cass could not keep the anxiety out of her voice. 'Where did you go?'

He gazed down at her, his eyes glittering. 'I had a blinding headache, a bloodstained suit and a need for solitude. After phoning you, I booked into the Hilton for the night.'

'Oh, Miguel,' she choked, 'I——' She took a step towards him, caught herself and turned quickly away. To say she was sorry would be an insult in its inadequacy.

'Cassandra?' She tensed at the note of strain in his voice. 'One thing you have not told me. Is that also a lie?'

She stood rigid, unmoving, not knowing what to say. To admit there was a kernel of truth, that meeting him *had* turned her whole life upside down and kindled within her a kaleidoscope of emotions and feelings such as she had never dreamed of was impossible. Not only would it be impertinent and embarrassing, but as there was no chance of her feelings ever being reciprocated, she would simply be inviting even greater pain. She had to lie to him for both their sakes. Yet the words would not come.

'Cassandra,' his voice was rough-edged, terse, 'answer me.'

Keeping her back to him, she swallowed the great lump in her throat. 'You are betrothed, Miguel,' with her eyes tight shut she forced the quiver out of her voice,

'Derek should have realised that under those circumstances the idea of ... anything between us is ... unthinkable.' Her head was leaden and her eyes felt hot and gritty.

The silence went on and on. Then softly, thoughtfully, he murmured, 'I see.' After another pause she heard his footsteps approaching and as she swung round, he was beside her, leaning across the desk. Riffling through various papers he selected several and taped them together neatly. 'This weekend is the fiesta of San Miguel,' he said conversationally. 'San Miguel is my birthplace and I am named for the saint. It is traditional for our family to return there to celebrate the festival. This year my parents will not be able to attend, so it is even more important that I go.'

'Of course.' Cass gave him a bright smile. 'I am more grateful than I can possibly say for all you have done, showing me the gems, the cutting-rooms, well, everything. And for your generous hospitality——'

'*Querida*,' he interrupted gently with a quizzical expression, 'why this little speech, delightful though it is?'

Her spine tingled at his use of the endearment. On Teresa's lips it sounded possessive, triumphant. Cass had never heard Miguel use it when speaking to his fiancée, yet he said it to her. She deliberately smothered the glimmer of hope and shifted awkwardly. 'If you are going away then naturally——'

'You will come too.'

She stared at him, stunned.

'It was part of your arrangement with my father, was it not?'

Cass shook her head. 'No. He simply suggested that if the possibility of seeing a fiesta arose, then I should take it.'

'Well.' Miguel spread his hands. 'It has and you shall.'

Surely he could see it wasn't that simple? 'I don't think——' she began.

'Enough. Always you are arguing with me.' His imperious tone froze her for a moment. But after an instant's shocked silence Cass's spirit was just about to reassert itself when he tossed the papers on to the desk and, clasping both her hands in his, held them against his chest. 'You *want* to go?' There was a quality in his intent gaze that sent a flood of warmth through her.

'It isn't——' She got no further as he covered her mouth with his fingertips.

'Do you *want* to go?' he repeated insistently.

Cass gave up. 'Do you need to ask?'

'Then it is settled.' He paused, tracing the outline of her face, then very gently he rubbed the back of his forefinger along the underside of her jaw. 'I will make it a very special time for you,' his voice was deep and vibrant, 'a time to remember always.'

Cass's heart turned over and she was suffused with a longing that was painful in its intensity. Then, suddenly, she was afraid, recalling Derek's taunt that Miguel would take advantage of any encouragement she might show him, and just as quickly discard her. While her body yearned for the solace only he could offer, she knew in her own heart that if she surrendered to her own desires and afterwards he rejected her, she would be utterly destroyed. She could not make love with him lightly and for him there could be no other way.

Sensing her withdrawal, he lifted one of her hands and laid it against his cheek. 'Relax, *querida*,' he ordered softly. 'You have nothing to fear.' He brought her hand to his mouth, but instead of kissing it, he bit her knuckle with infinite gentleness, sending a shaft of exquisite pleasure through her. 'Have you not branded me a man of honour?' His voice held several strange inflections that Cass's over-worked brain could not interpret.

Tension flickered between them like lightning before a summer storm. Beneath the material of his suit Cass could feel the rhythmic pounding of Miguel's heart. Unable to tear her eyes from his, she saw in their dark depths a naked, leaping flame of desire. Her breath caught in her throat as a fine trembling began deep inside her.

With a strangled oath forced between gritted teeth, Miguel dropped her hand and turned away, raking an unsteady hand through his hair, then rubbing the back of his neck. He cleared his throat, keeping his face averted. 'Benito is going to our mines today. I think it would be a good idea if you went with him. That was part of your plan and it will get you out of the house for several hours.'

Cass realised at once it was for the best. 'Thank you,' she whispered, still finding it hard to breathe.

'I have to fly to Texas,' he began, 'so——'

'Texas?' Cass repeated in surprise. Then she remembered. 'Your father—has something happened?' she asked with swift concern.

Miguel's profile was bleak. 'I telephoned the Institute last night. The operation has been brought forward to this afternoon. I must be with my mother until it is over and we know—the outcome. It is unlikely I will get back before dinner, but do not worry.' He glanced over his shoulder at her. 'You will face no unpleasantness. I will ensure that Teresa curbs her tongue.' A cynical smile lifted one corner of his mouth. 'As she intends that Prentice shall accompany us to San Miguel, I foresee no problems.'

Cass gazed at him in perplexity. No problems? After all that had happened? Certainly Teresa would toe the line if it meant she would get what she wanted, but what *did* she want? And what about Derek? What would *he* do now?

As if reading her thoughts Miguel's eyes narrowed. 'Prentice is not a complete fool. His pride has been dented but, like the jackal, he has a strong sense of self-preservation. It will be made crystal clear that if he troubles you in any way or threatens your job, he will be thrown off the Ibarra estates. I shall also make sure he finds it impossible to buy gems, cut or uncut, from any source whatsoever in Mexico.' His tone was merciless, his expression glacial, and Cass knew that on no account could she allow Miguel to discover she had already lost her job. She had no doubt he would carry out his threat. But it would be Matthew Prentice, Derek's father, who would be hurt most, and she refused to be the cause. Matthew had enough burdens to bear without seeing the business he had built up from nothing to a small but internationally renowned company dragged through the mud. What happened when Derek took over was Derek's concern, but right now Matthew was still in charge and for as long as he remained so she would do nothing to damage him or the name of the company. She sighed sadly. Derek was doing that all by himself.

Miguel picked up his papers and moved so that the desk was between them. 'Now please go,' he was brusque. 'We leave in twenty minutes.' He did not look up.

Cass fled to her room. After repairing her make-up, aware even as she applied lipstick and blusher that she was trying to create a façade behind which to hide, she twisted her tumbling hair into a knot and pinned it on top of her head. Sketch-book, pencils, notepad, purse were tossed into the capacious shoulder bag she always used on research expeditions.

The routine movements required little concentration and left her free to range back over those minutes spent with Miguel. Such precious minutes.

She tried desperately to banish the longing. For

herself and Miguel there could be nothing. Yet that was
a lie. It existed. It was there, flaring white-hot between
them. But it was unspoken and must remain so. Its
depths would never be plumbed, its heights never
scaled. It was a glow in which she warmed herself and a
conflagration which could devour her.

She had waited all her life to fall in love, believing it
was something that happened gently and gradually over
weeks and months of growing closeness.

Nothing in her imagination had prepared her for this
maelstrom of torture and ecstasy. Was it love that had
blown her life apart with all the subtlety and finesse of a
bomb? Could there be anything more foolish than to fall
in love with a man not free to love her?

Anguish pierced her with jagged blades. Pressing her
lips tightly together to stop their quivering, she picked
up her bag and a scarf and, with a final glance around,
opened the door, catching her breath as she almost
collided with Miguel.

He had changed his suit for one of dove-grey. His pale
pink shirt and maroon striped tie emphasised the bronze
tone of his skin and the blackness of his hair. Cass's heart
contracted at the sight of him.

'Do you want coffee before we go?' he asked as they
went downstairs.

'No, thanks.' She couldn't have swallowed a thing.

'Right. Go on out to the chopper. I'll pick up my
briefcase and we'll be on our way.' Though he did not
smile, his eyes were warm. 'Consuelo,' he shouted,
moving towards the study. The housekeeper appeared
almost at once. 'Tell Señor Morelos I'll arrange a charter
helicopter to pick him up in about an hour.'

Cass enjoyed every minute of the all-too-brief
journey. She had never imagined using helicopters with
the same casualness as taxis, yet it clearly saved Miguel
an enormous amount of time.

They both donned sunglasses and Miguel put headphones over her ears and helped her adjust the tiny microphone so that they could talk to one another while he listened for air traffic information.

Most of the time she looked out of the windows, enjoying the sound of his voice as he indicated in the far distance the ice-clad peak of the extinct volcano, Popocatapetl, the smoking mountain. She followed his pointing finger and saw an eagle, wingtips upcurving as it soared, spiralling slowly up into the cloudless sapphire sky. The harsh sunlight was almost too bright to bear despite her glasses, and above the barren hills the air shimmered.

Benito greeted her with shy pleasure and seemed delighted when Miguel announced she would accompany him to the mines. He did not ask where Derek was and Cass guessed he was not sorry she was alone.

'Benito, do you notice something strange?' Miguel eyed Cass thoughtfully. 'Miss Elliott designs beautiful jewellery, yet wears none.'

'Not so strange,' Cass smiled. 'I cannot afford to buy most of what I make. But I do have some earrings of my own design, and a dress ring.'

'Why you no wear them?' Benito asked, openly curious. 'My wife she love rings. She wear on every finger.'

'Force of habit, I suppose,' Cass shrugged. 'It's not safe when I'm working with stones and metals, and when I'm designing they distract me.'

'You have opals?' Benito asked.

'No.' With a pang Cass remembered the magnificent fire opal Miguel had shown her. What a fabulous ring that would make. With an inward sigh she pushed the thought away. It was not for sale, and if it were she would probably not be able to afford it, especially now that she was without a regular job.

'Then you must design one, very special, for reminding of your visit to us,' Benito decided, nodding vigorously.

Cass merely smiled.

'As a matter of interest,' Miguel said casually over his shoulder as they entered his office, 'assuming you are not working to a commission, how do you decide what size to make your rings?'

Cass watched him unlock a wall safe concealed by a picture. Opening the small but very thick door, he withdrew several wads of dollar bills and handed them to Benito, who stacked them neatly in a stiff, black briefcase. 'Well, provided the shank is reasonably wide I make them to an L, my own size, so that I can try them for balance and comfort. They can easily be enlarged if necessary. May I ask what the money is for?'

'Wages for the men.' He turned to Benito. 'Jose and Martinez will shadow you today.' He glanced at his watch. 'You had better get going. Enjoy your day, Miss Elliott.' He inclined his head politely, but his eyes gleamed with a warm intimacy that brought the blood surging to her cheeks.

'Thank you, Señor Ibarra,' she returned with equal politeness. Then, hesitantly, she added, 'I hope all goes well with your father. Waiting will be the hardest part, but I'm sure your presence will comfort your mother enormously.'

Surprise flickered briefly across his face, and he stared hard at her for a long moment. 'Thank you,' he said gravely and seemed about to add something, but deciding against it, he merely nodded once more.

They reached the opal mine in just under an hour. The car's air conditioning made the journey more comfortable than it would otherwise have been. Benito was a fast but expert driver and Cass was happy to listen to him talk as they bounced over the winding track through the eastern hills. A trail of thick, yellow-brown dust hung in the air to mark their passage.

Carrying one of the safety-helmets Benito had taken from the back of the car, Cass followed him into a compound patrolled by two swarthy, roughly dressed men carrying shot-guns. However, their unfriendly scowls were banished by beaming grins as Benito introduced her.

While he dealt with the wages, Cass wandered around the compound, looking at the little group of sheds, the barbed-wire fencing and the heavy gate with its chains and padlock.

When Benito emerged from re-locking the case in the car, she followed him through a narrow fissure in the hillside.

They picked their way carefully down a narrow tunnel, the light from their torches bouncing off the purplish-brown rock. The tunnel curved round and Cass could hear the sound of voices and the clink of hammers.

Benito called out in Spanish. Someone answered and a few moments later they came upon four men.

Stripped to the waist, their faces and bodies streaked with dust and sweat, they grinned appreciatively at Cass, their teeth flashing white in the light of lamps hanging from nails hammered into the rock face.

Cass shone her torch around while Benito talked to the men and shuffled beneath a lot of questions and banter in a dialect far too quick and accented for her to understand. Between them and the men stood an old and dented wheelbarrow lined with coarse sacking. More sacks lay in a heap on the tunnel floor. Curious to see what was in the barrow, Cass took a step forward. Her foot turned on a rut in the floor and she bumped against the wall. The beam of her torch lit up the tunnel roof. Cass gasped aloud. Like a million rainbows the whole roof blazed with incandescence. Pinpoints of orange and crimson dazzled amid streaks of emerald green and electric blue.

'Is fantastic, no?' Benito was grinning like a Cheshire cat, relishing Cass's stunned amazement.

'Oh, it's ... it's ... *beautiful*,' she breathed, gazing awestruck at the layer of opal that reached almost to both sides of the tunnel roof.

As they returned to the car Benito told her how the men had discovered the layer, had tunnelled along beneath it, and were now carefully breaking it away from the mother rock. 'Is very high grade. Our cutters will make many, many beautiful gems.'

They stopped for lunch in a small town that reminded Cass of a cowboy movie set. A huddle of clapboard buildings including a general store and a saloon lined the dusty main street, and a small white church stood in a square at one end. The peasants going about their business seemed unsurprised to see them. When Cass queried this Benito explained that the town was a tourist attraction, having been used as a background for several classic westerns.

The food they were served in the litle cantina was delicious. Instead of pulque, a kind of fermented liquor made from Maguey, Cass drank juice. Cool and delicious, it slid down her parched throat like nectar and Benito told her it came from the fruit of a cactus known to the Americans as prickly pear. It was mid-afternoon by the time they started back.

When they arrived at the *hacienda*, Cass told Benito how much she appreciated the time and care he had taken to explain everything to her. He blushed furiously and muttered '*De nada*'. But he was clearly delighted she had enjoyed herself so much.

Never had Cass welcomed a shower as much as she did that evening. By the time she emerged, having washed her hair as well, she felt revitalised and capable of coping with anything.

Neither Miguel nor Don Diego returned for dinner. With only herself, Teresa and Senōra Morelos present, the meal was eaten in virtual silence.

Out of courtesy she asked after Derek. But Teresa, allowing that he was now conscious and resting comfortably with no ill-effects other than a headache, seemed disinclined to talk.

Señora Morelos enquired how she had spent her day. But as Cass began to tell her, shock and disapproval spread across the older woman's face. Recalling Teresa's views of working women, which had plainly originated with her mother, Cass recognised the pointlessness of continuing and said simply that it had been both interesting and instructive.

Don Diego arrived back at nine, but it was after ten when Miguel returned. Cass was on her way up to bed when he came in through the front door. He looked tired and strained and her heart went out to him.

'So you are back at last.' There was a querulous note in Teresa's voice as she came out into the hall to greet him. 'It has been so boring without you, Miguel. I shall be glad to get to San Miguel and see some fun.' She put up her face for him to kiss.

Cass turned away quickly and continued quietly up the stairs, only to hear him call her name. She stopped, glancing back over her shoulder.

'Excuse me one moment,' he murmured to Teresa and started up the stairs towards Cass. 'I will not keep you, doubtless you are tired,' he called. 'I wish only to hear that your trip provided some useful information.'

Teresa tossed her head. 'Always work,' she snorted and flounced back into the sitting-room. Cass stared after her, deeply shocked. Miguel *must* have told her, yet she had not even mentioned his father.

As he reached Cass, Miguel lowered his voice. 'Ride with me in the morning.' It was both command and invitation.

Cass stared at him, biting her lip, torn. She wanted to so much, yet was it not asking for trouble, especially with emotions running so high?

'*Please,*' he grated.

Cass's eyes widened. To ask did not come easily to Miguel Ibarra.

'We will not talk. I will not touch you. Just be with me.'

She nodded and he turned away. 'Miguel?' Without thinking she laid her hand on his arm, withdrawing it quickly as his gaze flickered downward.

'Your father—the operation?'

His eyes met hers. 'So far all is well. The operation was a success, but he is very weak. The next few days will tell.'

Cass nodded. 'And your mother?'

'She is already planning his homecoming.' He grinned and she smiled back.

He kept his word. Sometimes she wondered if he had forgotten she was there. Then, suddenly he would turn, his eyes dark with a brooding intensity that made her quiver inside.

Side by side they stood and watched the sunrise, and once again Cass felt a great sense of awe, as though she were part of some ancient and terribly important ritual. Then he held the mare while she mounted and they rode back in silence. Yet the atmosphere between them had undergone a subtle change and Cass was imbued with a sense of peace and well-being. If there could be nothing more than this, just being with him was a joy she would not willingly forfeit. She would pay later, when she returned to England, in loss and loneliness. But for the first time in her life she was totally alive, and watching him, tall and relaxed on the spirited Diablo as he led the way down the track, she was fiercely glad to know Miguel Ibarra.

They re-entered the house together, a risk on his part that surprised and concerned her. In the hall he stopped, caught her hand and, turning it over, pressed his mouth to her palm. 'Thank you,' he whispered with a fleeting smile, then gave her a gentle push towards the stairs. 'Go along. I have work to do,' and he disappeared into his study.

Cass crept up the stairs. The house was still silent. As she reached the top and started towards her room, Derek's door opened.

CHAPTER NINE

CASS was immediately tense, anticipating Derek's demand to know the reason for her being about so early. After what had happened the previous day, would he be prepared to forgive and forget? Somehow she doubted it.

But to her amazement it was Teresa who emerged backwards through the door. Clad in a rose-pink négligé of lace over chiffon, her ebony hair cascaded down her back. She closed the door softly then jumped, visibly startled, as she caught sight of Cass.

'Good morning.' Good manners demanded she say something, but Cass would have gone straight to her room had Teresa not caught her arm.

'What are you doing? Are you spying on me?' Teresa whispered shrilly, then her gaze fell to Cass's dust-streaked boots and her over-bright eyes sharpened with curiosity. 'Where have you been?'

Cass chose her words with care. 'I woke early and went out for some air.' She would say no more than was absolutely necessary.

'Have you seen Miguel?' Teresa's tone was a mixture of nervousness and suspicion, but beneath it ran a current of excitement. Cass felt a stirring of dread.

'When I came in I saw him go into his study,' she answered truthfully.

Teresa's relief was plain, but Cass wasn't sure of its cause until the girl said smugly, 'It is his custom to wake me when he returns from his ride. He leads such a busy life, those moments of privacy are very special to us both. It would disappoint him to find me already up.'

It was on the tip of Cass's tongue to point out that he might be even more disappointed to find her in another man's room, especially in her present state of undress. But she said nothing, merely inclining her head, and started towards her room.

Teresa must have guessed her thoughts for she tightened her grip on Cass's arm. 'I thought he called out.' She fluttered a graceful hand towards Derek's door. 'Last night he started to run a fever. I was very concerned in case of the concussion.'

'Of course,' Cass murmured, wondering how Teresa could have heard a babble of delirium along twenty feet of passage between two closed doors. 'Is he still feverish?'

Teresa shook her head. 'Praise God and all the saints, it has gone.' Her creamy skin was tinged with pink. 'He is a strong man and has now fully recovered.'

'Good.' Cass hesitated for a moment, then decided to speak. 'Teresa, be careful.'

The other girl's chin tilted and her eyes flashed. 'What is this? What are you saying?'

Cass wished she hadn't started but there was no going back now. 'Just don't take anything Derek says too seriously.'

'You are afraid of what he may say about you?' Teresa sneered.

'I don't give a damn what he says about me,' Cass retorted in exasperation. 'I'm talking about the flattery he will pour over you, and the flirting——'

'Aaahh,' Teresa smiled mistily. 'To flirt adds a little spice to life, no? And what man would not be proud that others admire his woman? You need not be concerned for me. Derek is fun. He makes me laugh. I will not lose Miguel because another man finds me desirable, if that is what you were hoping,' she added slyly.

Cass could think of no reply to such confidence.

Realising she was wasting her time she lifted one shoulder in a half-shrug.

'Besides,' Teresa continued with saccharine sweetness, 'Miguel will never know about this morning, unless you choose to tell him. And if you did that it would put you in a very bad light, would it not? A woman scorned? Jealous? Bearing malice? But of course you are none of those things,' she said smoothly, 'you and I both know that.'

Cass gazed at the girl for a long moment. 'Derek did not dump me,' she said with quiet firmness. 'It was the other way round.'

'Of course,' Teresa soothed. 'Let us say no more about it. Tell me, do you have a long dress with you?'

The question surprised Cass. 'No. Why?'

'It is custom at the fiesta to dress in one's prettiest evening clothes and join in the dancing and celebrations.' she snapped her fingers. 'I have an idea! Myself, I shop in Mexico City, but there are some very good places in Queretaro, not too expensive. We will travel in with Miguel and while he is at his office, we will go and buy you something suitable.'

Oh, I don't think it's nec——' Cass began, but Teresa was bubbling with enthusiasm.

'Of course it is. This is your first fiesta, you may never see another, so you must honour it by looking as pretty as you can. That way you will enjoy it more.'

A special time, Miguel had said. A time to remember always. Joy and anguish were inextricably mingled as she thought of him. She had already recognised Teresa's invitation as a bribe in return for which she was to remain silent about this meeting.

A strange recklessness possessed her. Teresa's exhortation that she must 'look as pretty as you can' did nothing to hide the younger girl's condescension and Cass saw quite clearly that Teresa fully expected to outshine her no matter what she wore.

Well, she would show her! She would show them all! Teresa's parents with their disapproving stares; Derek who had thought to browbeat and blackmail her; Teresa whose sophistication and egotism made her totally insensitive to others; and Miguel. Miguel with whom she was hopelessly in love.

She would scintillate, she would glow. Iridescent as an opal, she would dazzle them all. Let him see what he was missing. She would flirt and have fun. Wasn't that what fiestas were for? If this was her first and last chance, she would make sure it was an occasion *none* of them forgot!

Teresa duly announced at breakfast that she simply had to go into Queretaro for some last-minute shopping. Then, as if struck by a brainwave, she turned the full force of her smile on Cass.

'Why don't you come with me? There are some nice little shops. I'm sure you would find something just right for the fiesta.'

Miguel's eyebrows lifted fractionally at this and he shot Cass a quizzical glance as she murmured that she would enjoy it.

Teresa whirled her through shop after shop, dismissing with an impatient flap of her hand one dress after another. Just what Teresa was looking for Cass wasn't certain. The dresses she quite liked Teresa emphatically rejected, while the ones Teresa favoured, usually bold reds and brilliant pinks, Cass knew would clash horribly with her hair and make her complexion appear sallow.

It dawned on her quite early in their expedition that Teresa was out to undermine her, to try and persuade her to buy something totally unsuitable. Realising this, Cass decided not to take any notice. She had no intention of buying anything she wasn't one hundred per cent certain about.

Now she was here she was enjoying herself. She

hadn't been shopping for clothes in a very long time and this was, after all, an out-of-the-ordinary purchase. She wondered briefly *why* Teresa was so bothered. Could it be her self-confidence was a fraction less solid than it appeared? Yet why should that be? Surely she had it all, beauty, wealth, doting parents, an indulged, secure and protected life and her future planned—Cass shied away from that and deliberately concentrated her attention on the rack of dresses in front of her.

Suddenly she saw it. This was the one. Cass lifted the dress down. To do so she had to reach past Teresa, who was extolling the virtues of a scarlet and yellow flowered print which made Cass think of dollops of tomato sauce on acres of scrambled egg. The harassed saleswoman, cowed by Teresa's impatient hauteur, stepped timidly forward, her face breaking into a smile.

'*¿Probarmelo usted?*' she gestured towards a curtained alcove. 'You try it?'

As Cass nodded, Teresa began to laugh. 'Cass, you cannot mean it. Not that thing? It's a rag.'

'It's the one I want,' Cass replied simply.

'But there are more shops to see. It is foolish to buy the first thing that catches your eye. Think how you'll regret it when you find something better.'

Cass smiled. 'There isn't anything better.'

'Well, it probably won't fit.'

'Then I'll alter it. But it will fit, you'll see.' Cass didn't know why she was so sure. But there wasn't a shred of doubt in her mind as she quickly stripped to bra and panties and stepped into the dress. She had zipped up the back then, on an impulse, piled her hair loosely on top of her head, leaving a few tendrils curling softly on her neck and in front of her ears, using grips from a little pot thoughtfully provided on the small shelf beside a packet of tissues. She lowered her arms and stared at her reflection for a long moment.

A vivid turquoise colour, the sleeveless pintucked bodice fitted her like a second skin. A deep frill, edged with matching broderie anglaise, framed the wide neckline and just covered her shoulders. A narrow sash, tied in a bow at the front, emphasised her slender waist and the deeply gored skirt had three wide pintucked frills. Against the blue-green, her skin seemed to glow and her eyes had a new brilliance. Its richness was a perfect foil for the golden fire of her hair. She pushed the curtain aside and stepped out.

'*¡Estupendo, señorita!*' The saleswoman beamed, then raised one finger. '*Con su permiso.*' She hurried to another rail and returned with a bouffant petticoat of white broderie Anglaise frills. Helping Cass into it, the woman quickly arranged the skirt over the top and stood back. Cass looked in the mirror. It was perfect. She turned round, looking over her shoulder to see the effect.

'It's beautiful,' she exulted.

'Well, I think you're making a mistake,' Teresa announced. 'I mean, *cotton*,' she made it sound like sackcloth, 'it's so unsophisticated.'

Perhaps that's why it suits me,' Cass said lightly as she went into the changing-room.

Teresa seemed to have lost all interest in shopping and Cass was content to acquiesce in her insistence that they return to the office to wait for Miguel.

Luisa brought them coffee and Cass was happy to sit in the reception area relaxing in the quiet comfort and watching people come and go. But Teresa quickly grew restive. Her high heels tapped briskly on the tiles as she crossed to the desk.

Cass's Spanish wasn't good enough for her to follow the entire conversation, but from odd words she gathered that Teresa was demanding to be allowed through to Miguel while Luisa regretted it was not possible.

It occurred to Cass to try and distract Teresa, to point out that Miguel was no doubt trying to clear as much as possible before they left for San Miguel. But she decided against it. If Teresa had not enough sense to realise that for herself, or if, in her selfishness, she chose to ignore it, anything Cass said would only worsen matters.

Eventually Miguel emerged. He saw her immediately and their eyes met. The contact lasted only a split second but it was enough to set her heart pounding.

Without even a greeting Teresa began at once to complain about Luisa. Miguel allowed her to finish, then, courteous but unapologetic, he explained that Luisa was simply following orders. His orders.

Teresa changed tactics and pouted, fawning over him with widened eyes, telling him breathlessly that she missed him when they saw so little of one another.

Cass was overcome with a wild desire to laugh at this theatrical display. Then she remembered what Teresa had said about Miguel waking her every morning after his ride. The laughter died in her throat and she looked away, fighting knifing pangs of jealousy.

'I see you were successful.' Miguel had approached and stood beside her chair. He indicated the large bag bearing the name of the dress shop.

'It's quite unsuitable, Miguel,' Teresa carped. 'I did try to——'

'Are you happy with your choice, Cassandra?' he asked, ignoring Teresa completely.

'It is exactly what I wanted,' she said quietly, meeting his dark gaze. As the electricity flickered between them she lowered her eyes swiftly, not daring to look longer.

'Then the fiesta will be enhanced by your presence.'

His voice was warm and she felt her colour rise. Teresa's irritation was palpable.

'Come, Miguel, if you are finished at last, let us go back to the hacienda. Where is Papa?'

'He will meet us at the helicopter. He is attending a meeting with his bankers.'

'More meetings?' Teresa sighed. 'When will the takeover be done with, Miguel? Papa will win, won't he?' Cass detected a faint thread of concern.

'It is not a simple matter of win or lose,' Miguel replied. 'Your father cannot stand alone against the big groups being formed by amalgamations of various textile companies. Maybe it would not be such a bad idea for him to sell out now and retire. He would make a handsome profit.'

'But he built the company himself from nothing,' Teresa objected. 'He has always said it was to remain in the family, to be handed down to his grandchildren, our sons, Miguel.'

Cass felt cold fingers close round her heart.

'A worthy sentiment,' Miguel observed drily. 'But I doubt it will keep the wolf from the door.'

'What do you mean?' Teresa snapped, frowning. 'Surely Papa doesn't have to sell if he doesn't want to?'

Cass bit her tongue. She realised she would be wasting her breath. Tempted though she was to explain that for a business to remain viable required updating of machinery and methods, increased output to meet demand, the ability to compete with cheaper imports, and healthy profits to cushion periodic recession, Teresa wouldn't have the faintest idea what she was talking about.

'He cannot go on the way he is.' Miguel stated the unpalatable truth gently.

'But if they force him out, and someone else is put in his place . . .' For the first time Teressa seemed to grasp what her father was up against. 'Miguel, it would kill him,' her voice wavered.

'It may come to that,' he allowed, almost reluctantly.

'How so?' she demanded, tears trembling on her darkened lashes. 'You say Papa has no choice.'

'There is a possibility of another company making an offer. If all aspects of the proposal are acceptable to your father, then it is feasible he could remain on the board of directors and continue to have a substantial say in the overall running of the company.'

Teresa's face lit up. 'Then of course he must accept this new offer.' She clutched his arm. 'Miguel, you must persuade him.'

He gently disentangled himself. 'Your father will make his own decision.' Cass detected a slightly grim note as he added, ' He will have much to consider.'

By the time they sat down to lunch Teresa had completely recovered and was a picture of vivacity which, Cass suspected, was more than partly due to Derek's presence beside her.

Apart from a slight pallor, Derek showed no ill-effects from either the alcohol or the blow to the back of his head. He was smartly but casually dressed in cavalry twill trousers, tweed sports jacket, a cream shirt and brown patterned tie. His shoes had a mirror gloss on them, his fair hair was neatly brushed and the scent of his aftershave wafted across the table. Talking with charm and wit, he appeared totally relaxed, but beneath the surface Cass sensed a suppressed excitement. She had seen him like this during the wheeling and dealing he used to secure business agreements and it made her deeply uneasy. He was behaving as if the last forty-eight hours had never happened. Surely he had learned *something* from the débâcle? It had been due only to Miguel's intervention that he had not ended up in jail.

As she watched him pass serving-dishes to Teresa with meaningful glances and murmured remarks that made her laugh and blush even as she playfully slapped his hand, it seemed to Cass that he was brazenly tempting Miguel and fate to do their worst.

Then it hit her. Surely Derek could not be the other

party interested in Teresa's father's business? No, she told herself firmly, it was impossible. He had no experience of textiles. Yet hadn't he always maintained that business was business whether you were selling cornflakes or carpets? Once he inherited his father's company it was his to do with as he liked. But *why* would he ... of course. If he bought into Morelos Textiles he would immediately have access to a network of contacts in Mexico which even Miguel's influence would not be able to deny him. And she realised now that Derek was capable of anything when it came to repaying what he saw as a slight.

She felt Miguel's gaze on her and glanced up. He was regarding her with a quizzical expression that contained an element of anger. It puzzled her until she realised she had been so busy watching Derek and Teresa that her lunch had grown cold. She lowered her eyes quickly and began to eat.

To her surprise and delight Miguel stipulated that she sit next to him for the journey. She expected Teresa to argue but she was too busy talking to Derek. As soon as all the luggage was stowed and everyone fastened into their seats, Señor and Señora Morelos with their backs to the cockpit, Teresa and Derek facing it, they lifted off and turned north-west towards San Miguel.

Magnificent scenery unrolled beneath them as they left the dry, agave-covered hills. Miguel pointed out places of interest. 'That is Real del Oro. It's almost a ghost town now.' She could hear him clearly through the headphones. 'The fabulous Descubridor vein of gold was discovered there in the eighteenth century by the Spaniards. For a while, as miners and prospectors flooded in from all over the world, there were almost fifty thousand people crammed into the town.'

In a beautiful mountain valley Cass saw another little town situated at the edge of an expanse of water that glistened in the sun-light. 'I wouldn't have expected to see a lake up here,' she remarked.

'It is not natural,' he told her, 'but one of a chain of artificial lakes which are part of a vast hydro-electric project. It is well stocked with fish, and any tourist brave enough to venture there can go boating or swim as well as try their luck with a rod.'

'Why should they need to be brave?' Cass watched him grimace.

'Because outside the main cities my countrymen have still not awoken to the fact that to attract tourists you have to offer facilities of a similar standard to those they have at home. All too often the accommodation that does exist is totally inadequate and badly maintained.'

'Perhaps the Mexican people simply do not want tourists,' Cass mused. 'There is often a high price to be paid for the money they bring into a country.'

He gave her a thoughtful look. 'How much I still have to learn about you.'

'Why bother?' she retorted lightly, turning her head away to stare out of the side window.

'Flippancy does not become you,' he chided. 'Nor is it necessary.'

'You think not?' She kept her head averted. 'Well, how much can you learn about me in the short time I shall be here?' She was torturing herself. But she had to face the truth. Twenty days was all she had, and the longer she stayed the more agonising would be her departure.

'What have you learned about me and yourself in the brief time since your arrival?' he responded.

She was silent as a kaleidoscope of images danced before her eyes. She shivered and grew warm again reliving fragments of the intense emotions she had experienced.

'Exactly,' he murmured in quiet triumph. 'Now tell

me why Prentice and Teresa deserved so much of your attention this morning.'

'Miguel,' she hesitated, diffident, 'aren't you worried? The way Teresa is encouraging Derek——'

'Teresa's behaviour is her own business,' he cut in, 'not mine, and certainly not yours.' His tone softened. 'Let it be *querida*'. He smiled at her. 'There is no cause for worry.'

Built on the slopes of Cerra de Montezuma overlooking the Laja river valley, San Miguel was thronged with people. Plazas and patios blazed with masses of flowers and the colourful costumes of the dancers. From all directions they came, streaming into the town, on foot, on muleback and in horse-drawn carts laden with baskets, pots, toys, hand-woven serapes, embroidered blouses, fruit and vegetables, all to be sold from the stalls being set up in every street and plaza.

Cass barely had time to take in the rows of tall houses faced with brown stucco or terracotta stone with wrought-iron balconies in front of the long windows.

Miguel broke the silence, pointing to a beautiful pink stone edifice in the central plaza. In front of it, circles of dancers swayed and bobbed. 'That is the church of San Miguel. It was originally a plain Franciscan building, but it was refaced by an illiterate Indian stonemason who also happened to be an architectural genius. He based his design on picture postcards of French cathedrals.'

'Who are they?' Cass leaned forward to point down at a group of striking-looking women in starched headdresses, white blouses thickly embroidered with floral designs, and purple skirts with a lace ruffle at the hem, who swayed gracefully to music played by a band comprising guitars, drums and maracas.

'Tehuantepec women,' Miguel replied. 'You would feel at home with them, they are noted for their beauty and their fierce independence.' He raised one dark brow and Cass couldn't help smiling.

'There's something in the air, isn't there, a sort of excitement.' She glanced at him and he nodded.

'The Mexicans are a formal people, not given to revealing their true feelings.' Cass listened intently. 'But during the fiesta there is a complete reversal of the reticence of everyday living. People get drunk, weep, laugh, make love, exchange confidences, and sometimes kill each other. It is an explosion of the soul. It cleanses, revitalises and touches the inner fires of the spirit. One does not leave a fiesta unchanged.'

Cass looked out of the window, blind to the colour and spectacle below, as a battle raged within her. Should she remain aloof, an observer rather than a participant, and so attempt to minimise the effect on her of all that was happening? Or, like a non-swimmer plunging off the high board, should she leap into the unknown and live each moment to the fullest, making the most of whatever came? The risks were enormous, but at least she would really have *lived*.

'Did you win, *querida*?' Rich with laughter and tenderness, Miguel's voice penetrated her reverie.

She looked at him and drew in a deep breath. 'Yes,' she announced. The air between them was charged.

'And?'

She spoke softly, 'There is always the possibility the sun may not rise tomorrow.'

His jaw tightened and a muscle twitched at the corner of his mouth. Slightly hoarse he said drily, 'The spirit of the fiesta has touched you already.'

'Is *that* what it is?' she asked, all wide-eyed innocence, and laughed aloud at his muttered oath. Beneath the banter the invisible cord that joined them thrummed with tension.

As he brought the helicopter down, she groaned.

'What is it now?' The laughter in his eyes belied his mock impatience.

'You know perfectly well.' Cass removed her glasses and stared out of the window. 'You might have warned me.'

Miguel switched off the engines and the rotors began to slow. Adopting his most imperious glare which moved her not one bit, he demanded, 'Where else would you expect me to live?'

'In a pyramid like any other emperor,' she retorted. 'You *implied* a "little place in the country" on the edge of a small town.'

'Well?' he said blankly.

'There was no mention of a palace!'

Miguel tilted his head on one side and appraised the sumptuous house standing in landscaped gardens that were a riot of colour. He had brought the helicopter down on a flagged circle in the centre of the lawn. 'Hardly that,' he demurred. 'Though we do have a swimming-pool,' he fell into the ingratiating whine of an estate agent, '... full-size ... heated ... with a complex of changing-cabins, showers, and bar. Plus a selection of swimsuits for guests who come unprepared.'

Cass pretended to consider. 'All right then,' she said wearily. 'I'll stay.'

'*Gracias, señorita.*' He stretched his mouth in an inane grin.

For Cass the contrast between the natural dignity and imposing demeanour of the Miguel she was used to and the clown he had suddenly become was too much and she was convulsed with laughter.

Miguel clipped both sets of headphones out of the way as the motor noise ceased. Cass was still chuckling.

'You two certainly seem to be enjoying yourselves,' Derek observed acidly.

'That is what the fiesta is about,' Miguel replied. 'I

hope you also will enjoy it.'

'Oh, I plan to,' Derek muttered, but Miguel was already out of the pilot's seat and walking towards the manservant who had come out to greet him.

The pulsing rhythm of a hundred different dances floated on the warm air. Firecrackers exploded and now and then a rocket shot skyward leaving a trail of red sparks.

In spite of its exquisite furnishing, cool spaciousness and priceless antiques, the house was no museum. It had the warm, welcoming atmosphere of a much-loved home.

Cass could hardly believe her room. It was enormous. The bed, a four-poster with curtains of silver and pearl brocade, looked large enough to accommodate a family. There was an enormous wardrobe and two large chests of intricately carved black wood. But the high ceiling and two long windows gave the room a light airiness that counterbalanced the heavy furniture.

As the maid insisted with smiling firmness on unpacking for her, Cass decided to go down for a swim.

Several costumes were arrayed on a shelf in the *cabaña*. Selecting an emerald one-piece, she quickly changed and pinning her hair up, padded out on to the terrace.

One end of the pool had wide, semi-circular steps leading down into the limpid blue water. Cass walked down until she was waist deep then glided forward in a leisurely crawl. The water was like silk. She had done two lengths and was half-way down a third when she was suddenly aware of someone beside her.

She missed her stroke and swallowed a mouthful. As she coughed and spluttered two strong arms slid around her.

'You will please not drink the pool,' Miguel ordered.

'You brute!' Still gasping, her eyes streaming, Cass

thumped his naked shoulder. 'You could scare a person to death.'

Miguel's arms held her close against his warm, muscular body. 'If I intended to kill you,' he grinned, his eyes narrowed to glittering slits, 'I could think of a much more ... satisfying method.'

Involuntarily her hands tightened on his shoulders. Blushing furiously, she stared as if mesmerised at the drops of water sparkling in the curling black hair that covered his broad chest. The quickening rhythm of his heartbeat echoed through her breast and she was vaguely surprised that the water around them wasn't boiling.

Obeying a reckless impulse, she fastened her legs around his hips, meaning to tip him off-balance and give him a retaliatory ducking. Only he didn't fall, and his deep-throated groan and the convulsive tightening of his arms as he crushed her hard against him revealed the extent of his arousal, and sent a liquid sweetness through her loins that made her shudder. She heard voices and Teresa's high-pitched laugh as she called to Derek.

'Miguel,' Cass whispered urgently, straightening her legs and pushing away from him.

He released her, but with evident reluctance. 'I must swim a while.' He shot her a look that made her blush even as she giggled, and set off in a powerful crawl that sent him through the water like an arrow.

Cass did a couple more lengths on her back, mainly to force the bone-melting weakness from her limbs, then climbed out and went to collect her things.

Teresa was stretched out on a lounger wearing a gold lamé bikini which was plainly not designed for swimming in, and did little to hide her opulent curves. Derek, in blue shorts, was smoothing protective lotion into her plump shoulders. He glanced up as Cass passed.

'Leaving already?' Malice lurked in his pale eyes as he

went on rubbing Teresa's back with a deliberate sensuality calculated, Cass knew, to worry her.

But if Miguel wasn't worried—however odd that seemed—why should she be? 'I think you missed a bit,' she said and walked past into the house, leaving Derek staring after her and Miguel still cleaving a relentless path through the sparkling water. Biting her lip on a smile, she went upstairs.

Setting down her perfume spray, Cass walked across to examine the total effect in the cheval-glass and sighed with happiness and anticipation. Her dress looked stunning. Cream low-heeled pumps peeped out from beneath the lowest frill. Her hair, arranged in a soft chignon, gleamed like burnished copper. She had used a subtle greeny-grey shadow on her eyelids and coral lip-gloss on her mouth. Blusher would have been superfluous. She positively glowed! She clipped on her coral and gold earrings and fastened a fine gold chain around her neck. She was ready.

She pushed open the double doors of the salon where they were all to meet before dinner. The room was empty save for Miguel who stood at the small bar adding ice-cubes to the whisky he had just poured.

But this was yet another Miguel, breathtakingly handsome in tight-fitting black suede trousers with a silver stripe at the side and a waist-length jacket of black leather embellished with silver embroidery which emphasised the width of his shoulders. A gunbelt was slung low on his lean hips with a silver-handled pistol in the single holster strapped to his right thigh. There were silver spurs on his black boots.

With his bronze skin and black hair curling thickly on the collar of a frilled white shirt, he was a strikingly dramatic figure, a piece of history come to life.

He picked up the crystal tumbler and as he raised it, caught sight of her in the lighted mirror behind the bar.

He was utterly still for a moment then, lowering the glass without touching a drop, he turned to face her.

Cass held her breath as his burning gaze swept her from head to toe.

'*Madre de Dios*,' he whispered, and her heart gave a great leap. 'Turn,' he commanded, gesturing with his free hand. Cass made a graceful pirouette, glancing shyly at him over her shoulder.

'Enough!' he grated, tossing back half his drink, his lip curling as the spirit burned its way down.

Cass was exultant. 'You like my dress, then?' she asked demurely.

'It is . . . acceptable,' he drawled.

'Oh, you——' She started towards him. 'One of these days, Miguel Ibarra——'

'A glass of sherry, perhaps?' he offered, cutting loudly across whatever she had been going to say, and following his gaze, she turned as Teresa, in a flamenco-style dress of black with scarlet flounces and a poinsettia in her sleek hair, came in with her parents and Derek.

After dinner they set off. It wasn't far to walk and the night air was balmy and redolent of woodsmoke and hot, spicy food.

Cass could make out at least four different tunes and doubtless there were dozens more being strummed, blown and beaten out by the seemingly tireless bands of musicians. Yet they did not clash but seemed to melt into a strange, multi-layered pulse-beat.

The streets were illuminated with row upon row of electric bulbs, slung between trees, across buildings and over the supporting frames of stalls. The sky exploded in bursts of colour as fireworks were set off. Women gossiped and laughed, men drank and sang, and children stared, round-eyed. Groups of Indian peasants with bare, calloused feet, blankets round their shoulders and straw hats set squarely on their heads, danced to the beat of a single drum, their brown, age-old faces immobile.

Derek, like Señor Morelos, was wearing a dinner-jacket, and Teresa's hand with its scarlet nails looked very white resting on his sleeve.

'Why did you have to wear that cowboy suit, Miguel?' she tutted.

'I would look out of place in the parade if I wore anything else,' he replied mildly.

'The parade,' she snorted, 'surely you should have outgrown such things. It is not in keeping with your position.'

'Teresa,' her father warned.

Miguel stopped and Cass saw his face granite-hard, its planes emphasised by the harsh artificial light and deep shadows.

'Throughout Mexico San Miguel is known as the cradle of independence. Were it not for the men who died fighting for freedom from Spanish rule, I would not *be* in my position. Besides, I believe in honouring the past. The *charros*, whose costume you scorn, are the backbone of this country and my roots here are much deeper than yours.'

'That is irrelevant,' she said at once. 'It is today that is important, not last year or three centuries ago.'

He gave the slightest of shrugs. 'Today we are at the fiesta, and I wear the *charro* costume to ride in the parade.'

Teresa snorted in exasperation, but Miguel had already moved on, dragging Cass with him through the milling crowd towards the central plaza.

As they looked at the displays of goods for sale many people spoke to Miguel and Cass noticed affection and respect from peasant and well-to-do alike. They strolled slowly past several groups of dancers, then a band of yellow-coated musicians a little distance away struck up a lively melody and Miguel guided Cass to the front of the crowd and stood close behind her, one hand resting on her waist.

The female dancers wore crinolined dresses of flounced layers edged with lace or ribbon that reached just below the knee. Their bodices had elbow-length puffed sleeves with a frill and a frilled collar. The male dancers wore *charro* outfits plus a huge sombrero.

'This dance is called *Jarabe Tapatio*,' Miguel murmured in her ear. 'It's a courting dance that originated in Guadalajara.'

Cass watched, fascinated as the couples moved round one another in set patterns, always maintaining a reserved distance from each other. As the dance moved towards its climax the music quickened, becoming gay and flirtatious. The men placed their sombreros on the ground and followed the girls as they danced round them. As each girl stooped to pick up the hat, her partner passed his right leg over her and the dance ended in a burst of clapping, laughter and noisy shouts as each couple stole a kiss behind the sombrero.

'I have to go now, to take my place in the parade,' Miguel said. 'You will be all right?'

'Of course.' She smiled up at him. 'I shall watch the dancing until it arrives.'

'Then you will watch me.'

'That sounds like a royal command,' she observed drily.

He raised one dark brow. 'Naturally.' And with a flashing grin he vanished into the darkness.

Cass glanced around. Señor and Señora Morelos were a few feet away deep in conversation with another couple in evening dress. On the other side, separated from her by a mother and her three daughters, Teresa was making eyes at Derek as she laughed at something he was saying.

The music started again and the dancers whirled into

an intricate series of steps. Cass watched, utterly
absorbed by the colour and the spectacle, unaware of
time passing.

When the dancers eventually stopped, the crowd
began to move away, seeking amusement elsewhere.
Cass was caught up in the press of bodies. She craned her
neck, but could see neither the Moreloses nor Teresa
and Derek.

The sound of a larger band playing martial music was
drawing nearer and the crowd began to move faster.
Cass was pushed along, nudged, elbowed and kicked.
Men, sucking on cans or bottles, staggered and fired
pistols into the air, laughing crazily. Swept along in this
torrent of excited humanity, Cass began to feel afraid.
She wanted to get out. She tried to fight her way free,
clutching her bag and cashmere shawl as if her life
depended on them.

Over the heads of the people she could see the parade,
led by a marching band in red jackets. Gloriously
decorated floats, banked with masses of flowers, trun-
dled slowly across the plaza. Then the jingling of spurs
and harness and the clopping of hooves echoed from the
tall buildings around the plaza. Instinctively Cass began
struggling towards it, towards Miguel.

But like a pack of hyenas, the drunken men recognised
Cass as both a stranger and a woman alone. She was
jostled and pawed. One man pushed a bottle towards her
face, saliva running down his chin as he urged her to
drink. She knocked it away and tried to run. Coarse,
excited laughter followed and she knew deadly fear.

CHAPTER TEN

THE parade was half-way across the plaza. Cass could see the riders about fifty feet away. Spurred on by terror she tried to fight her way forward. But the crush of bodies was impenetrable and the noise deafening.

Then she saw Miguel. He was on the side nearest her, third in the column. She shouted but could not even hear her own voice above the din.

A rough hand gripped her shoulder forcing her round. The man with the bottle had followed her. His loose, wet mouth stretched in a leer that revealed blackened teeth and his small eyes glittered with feverish excitement. With all her strength Cass pushed him away. He stumbled, falling backwards. All around people laughed, then ignored them both.

'Miguel! Help me!' Cass screamed, at the top of her lungs, stretching her arms towards him.

She saw him stiffen. He stood in his stirrups, scanning the crowd.

'Miguel! Here, I'm here!' Her voice cracked and her throat was raw, but he heard her. Breaking out of the formation, he set his horse at the crowd, scattering them left and right.

She was sobbing with relief, tears streaming down her face as he reached her. His face thunderous, he leaned down and swept her up behind him.

'Hold on to me,' he commanded. 'I will take you home.'

All around them the crowd cheered and shouted. Cass fastened her arms around his waist and buried her face against his broad shoulders.

By the time they reached the house she had regained a little of her composure but still trembled uncontrollably.

Miguel dismounted quickly and held up his arms to her. As she fell into them, she sensed barely controlled anger emanating from him.

'I'm sorry,' she whispered, her mouth quivering. 'But I was so scared——'

'Quiet.' He was brusque, and she fell silent as he bellowed for one of the servants. A man came running and Miguel handed him the reins, issuing a stream of orders. The man nodded quickly and led the horse away at a trot.

With his arm around her shoulders, Miguel supported Cass into the salon. Her knees felt like jelly and she clung to him with one hand. In the other she still clutched her bag and cashmere shawl like talismans. She sank down on to the brocaded sofa and he went straight to the bar, returning with a glass of brandy which he thrust into her hands.

'Drink it,' he rapped.

The rim rattled against her teeth as she took a sip, shuddering as the fiery spirit burned her raw throat. She raised her eyes and tried to smile, to reassure him that she was all right now. But to her utter dismay scalding tears filled her eyes, brimmed over and dripped off her chin. She lowered her head quickly, pressing her lips tightly together to stop their trembling, clutching the brandy glass between white-knuckled hands as her chest heaved on a muffled sob.

Muttering an oath, Miguel seized the glass, heedless of the antique brocade as the fine old brandy fell in scattered drops on to the gold material. Slamming it down on a nearby table, he yanked Cass to her feet, his hands grasping her shoulders with painful strength.

'Don't,' he rasped, his expression anguished, and folding his arms about her, crushed her to him. 'Don't,

Cassandra. I cannot bear to see you weep.'

She tried to push him away, her movements automatic, self-protective, conscience and instinct combining to warn her they were on dangerous ground. But he ignored her efforts, pressing his lips to her hair, her forehead, her temple and the side of her neck. 'No,' she whispered hoarsely.

Raising his head a fraction, with gentle fingers he lifted her chin. Their eyes met, hers tear-washed, vulnerable, his heavy-lidded and smoke-dark.

'Cassandra.' Her name vibrated in this throat then his mouth claimed hers, warm and briefly tender. Suddenly the dam burst. The crackling electricity and unspoken desire, the pent-up emotions both had tried to deny combined in an elemental torrent to sweep away everything but the moment.

As his mouth grew more demanding, so his hands moved over her body with a possessive intimacy that made her shiver with helpless delight. She moaned softly, clinging to his shoulders as his hands slid down over her hips forcing her hard against him, holding her there with arms like steel hawsers. His body was taut, trembling with his need for her. Melting, boneless, she moulded to him in a fever of mounting excitement. Her lips parted to his probing tongue and her blood roared in her ears as her heart pounded with such force it threatened to burst from her body. His breathing harsh and ragged, Miguel was a man almost beyond control.

The front door slammed. The sound of raised voices froze them for an instant then they sprang apart. Cass's legs simply gave way, and she collapsed on to the sofa, head bowed, hands clasped tight as she struggled for control.

Cursing with quiet and bitter fluency, Miguel strode to the bar and poured himself a brandy with hands that were not entirely steady. The salon doors flew open and

Teresa stormed in followed by Derek.

'How could you make such an exhibition of yourself!' she cried.

Cass's head flew up. She winced and moistened her lips, only to realise that Teresa's wrath was not directed at her, but at Miguel.

'What will all our friends think?' Teresa's fists were clenched, and there were hectic patches of colour on her cheek bones. 'You playing the gallant knight to a stupid English girl who has caused trouble ever since she arrived.'

'Teresa!' His voice was a whipcrack and his anger terrifying to behold. 'I answer to *no one*.' His words fell like pebbles into a still pool and in the shocked silence the ripples spread. 'You are a guest in my house, but you may leave whenever you wish.'

'*I* leave?' she shrieked. 'I have a *right* to be here. We are to be married, you and I. It is *she* who must leave,' she pointed a stabbing finger at Cass who felt deathly cold, 'that ... that ...' She turned and collapsed against Derek, sobbing wildly.

Miguel was unmoved. 'You abandoned her, you and Prentice. There is a fever, a delirium that infects the people at this time.' His tone was glacial, relentless. 'You know that, Teresa! You have seen it for yourself. Yet the two of you deserted——'

'Steady on, Ibarra,' Derek broke in, 'you can't blame Teresa. If Cass chooses to go wandering off on her own, it's nobody's fault but hers if she gets into trouble. For all you know she may have done it deliberately.' His mouth twisted in sly cynicism and he darted a glance of pure venom at Cass who recognised that he would grab every opportunity to discredit her, knowing she would not stoop to his tactics to hit back. 'After all, it got her what she wanted, didn't it?'

As Miguel, his face an impenetrable mask, turned to

Derek, Diego Morelos hurried in followed by his wife. '¿Que hay? What is all this crying and shouting?'

Teresa pulled away from Derek and hurled herself at her father, who rocked backwards beneath the impact. 'Papa! Miguel is so unkind! He shames me in front of everyone.'

'Hush, hush now, chiquita,' Diego comforted his daughter, patting her plump shoulder. 'It is nothing but a lovers' tiff. Soon you will be married and all this silliness will be forgotten.' He looked over Teresa's head. 'Perhaps Meestair Prentice, you will pour a small brandy for my daughter and myself. And something for my wife if she wishes it,' he added as an afterthought.

'Coming right up.' Derek's brightly artificial chirpiness did nothing to dispel the tension.

'Miguel,' Diego met his host's stony gaze, 'my daughter means everything to me. It may be I have indulged her a little too much, but,' he looked fondly at the girl in his arms and gave a helpless shrug, 'what father, indeed what man, could deny such beauty?' Teresa preened. 'She is a precious jewel who deserves a setting worthy of her. If she is a little wayward it is only her lively spirit which needs a firm hand to guide and control it. Miguel, it is time a date was set for your marriage.'

'Oh, Papa!' Teresa squealed happily and threw her arms around her father's neck.

Derek looked up from pouring the brandy to shoot Cass a glance of malicious triumph.

Cass felt as though she were falling into a black, bottomless pit. Echoing in her mind she heard Miguel's words . . . 'a fever, a delirium that affects people at this time'. She had been touched by it, held in thrall by the fiesta's spell, heedless of the future, living only for the moment. And each moment had been filled with Miguel. Unconsciously she raised an unsteady hand to her lips, still feeling the heat of his breath and the pressure of his mouth. Oddly light-headed, she felt the last faint glimmer of hope die. Now there was only paralysing despair as Miguel spoke.

'Diego, you are right.' He sounded grimly determined. 'What better time than this to settle the matter once and for all. Come, we will speak privately.' And without a backward glance he strode out of the salon, a tall, imposing figure, his regal bearing lending even greater dignity to his black and silver *charro* costume.

Teresa, her tears rapidly drying, was laughing and talking excitedly with her mother. Derek handed them each a measure of brandy, then lifted his own glass. 'A toast to the beautiful bride,' he proclaimed. 'And to the beautiful bride's beautiful mother!' He bowed smartly to Señora Morelos, who smiled and simpered.

Gathering the remnants of her dignity around her, Cass stood up. Picking up her bag and shawl from the corner of the sofa, she started towards the door. It took all the will-power she could muster to hold her head high and not run.

Hadn't she known, deep in her heart, that something like this would happen? Her pain was her own fault, she could blame no one else. She loved a man bound to someone else. All her dreams, her half-formed hopes and wild yearnings had contained no more substance than the mists that veiled the valleys at night only to be dissolved by the rising sun.

Miguel was her sun. For a while her soul had blossomed in his warmth. But he was also the eagle, soaring far beyond her reach, leaving her earthbound and alone.

She had to say *something*. Courtesy and her own pride demanded it. Her throat, still sore, was stiff with grief, and her voice little more than a hoarse whisper. 'I wish you every happiness, Teresa.'

The girl swung round, her eyes narrowed and full of spite. 'I do not need good wishes from *you*,' she spat.

Cass flinched and Derek grinned. Señora Morelos stared into her brandy glass.

'You have them nonetheless,' Cass murmured painfully. 'Good night.'

No one answered. Teresa turned her back in a calculated snub. As Cass crossed the hall she heard laughter then Derek's voice, '. . . quite pathetic really.'

Closing her door, Cass leaned against it. She felt unutterably weary. She walked slowly over to the bed and taking off her dress and petticoat, laid them on the counterpane. As she fingered the turquoise frills, her face crumpled and helpless tears slid down her cheeks. Such stupid, *stupid* dreams.

She picked up her velour robe. And what now? She was clearly unwelcome here. Derek and Teresa were actively hostile and the Moreloses barely polite. Only Miguel had sought her company and treated her—as what? A friend? No, the sexual tension that vibrated between them mocked mere friendship. But nor had he taken advantage of their mutual attraction to become her lover. Unable to restrain himself entirely, he had gone no further than kissing her. And how his kisses had stirred her, fanning the flow of newly awakened desire to white heat. He wanted her, she knew that, and she wanted him. But he had chosen Teresa and the marriage date was being set at this very moment.

How could she stay here now? How could she bear to see Miguel every day and pretend she felt nothing? And if he wanted to be alone with her, would she be able to deny him or herself? Yet what damage would be done by such furtiveness? There was only one thing she could do.

Dropping her robe, she crossed quickly to the wardrobe and took out her emerald Viyella shirt, a pair of chocolate-brown stretch slacks and a matching cable-knit sweater. Once dressed she unpinned her hair and shook it free, letting it fall about her shoulders.

Her tears had dried and her eyes felt hot. Concentrating on the physical act of packing her case kept her thoughts at bay, thoughts too painful to bear. There was a point beyond which agony became meaningless and an automatic survival reflex took over. Cass had reached it. Her decision to leave had brought a strange peace to her. Part of her had died and nothing would ever hurt as much again.

As she snapped the case shut there was a soft knock on the door. She tensed.

'Sí?'

'Con supermiso, Señorita,' the maid's voice filtered through the door. 'Don Miguel ask if you like something to eat, or hot drink maybe?'

His thoughtfulness was like a knife turning in her heart. 'No, thank you.' Cass fought to control her voice. 'I wish only to sleep. I—I have taken a pill.'

'Sí, señorita. At what time you like your breakfast?'

Cass thought rapidly. 'Not before nine.' She would be out of reach by then, the break clean and final.

'Gracias, señorita. Buenas noches.'

Her footsteps receded and Cass let out a long shuddering breath. Tearing a sheet from her notebook, she picked up her pencil with shaking fingers and, after a moment's hesitation, wrote four words. Signing the note simply 'C', she folded it, addressed it to Miguel and propped it up on the chest where it would be easily seen. Then, after a final look round to make sure she had forgotten nothing, Cass snapped off the light. Quietly easing the armchair round to face the window, she curled her legs under her and stared out at an inky sky streaked with firework flashes of orange, emerald, silver and gold. Gun shots echoed across the valley. Laughter, singing and the ceaseless rhythm of drums and guitars were borne away on the night wind.

A little while later Cass heard Derek, Teresa and her mother coming upstairs, busy making plans for the following day. They separated to their rooms with many 'Good nights.'

An hour after that she heard Miguel and Don Diego. They paused for a moment on the landing. Her fingers curled on the chair arms and she held her breath. There was a murmur of voices, then doors closed and there was silence.

Cass waited another hour before rising stiffly from the chair. Tying a scarf over her head to hide her hair, she picked up her boots and her suitcase and stole silently out of the house.

Keeping to the well-lit streets, she made her way to the railway station. The ticket office was empty and locked. She would have to pay on the train. Two Indian women, bundled in several layers of clothing, squatted by a wall. An official in a shabby uniform and cap hauled a squeaking trolley loaded with wooden crates into the middle of the platform, then ambled away.

The first grey streaks of dawn were beginning to brighten the darkness when the train arrived. As it clattered and swayed through the mountains and valleys the sun rose and a new day was born. Cass closed her eyes, unable to look.

Exhaustion took over and she must have dozed for it was with a start that she woke and realised they had reached Queretaro. Her head ached and her throat was parched. Clutching her case she stumbled down on to the platform and joined the crush heading for the exit. There was a small hiatus while she fumbled for money to pay her fare, and was jostled and pushed by others waiting to get past. Then she was out of the station.

Hailing a taxi, she gave the address of Miguel's office.

As they drove through the crowded streets Cass glanced at her watch. The maid would be taking her breakfast up any moment now. Soon Miguel would know she had gone. Would he be angry that she had left in such a manner? Surely he would understand that she could no longer face the combined forces of the Morelos family plus Derek?

It was foolish to pretend Miguel had no knowledge of her feelings for him. They had been too strong to deny and too powerful to contain. But surely he must see that by leaving she was sparing them both further shame or embarrassment. Not that she was ashamed of her love for him. But to have remained in his house, hoping for a few crumbs in the form of a stolen kiss or precious moments alone with him, while preparations were being made for his marriage to Teresa, would have degraded them both. She had *had* to leave.

Perhaps he would understand and be grateful. What she had to do next would tax the ability of a professional actress. As the cab drew up outside the building, Cass swallowed hard and stretched her mouth into some semblance of a smile. Taking a deep breath she walked into the reception area. Luisa smiled. 'Good morning, Mees Elliott.'

'Good morning. May I speak to Benito Suarez, please?'

'Benito?' Luisa repeated, sounding surprised.

'Yes. Is he not in yet? Oh,' Cass suddenly remembered, 'everything is all right, isn't it? His wife, I mean. The baby——'

'Yes, yes all is well. There is still some time to go,' Luisa reassured her and smiled again, 'Benito has difficult pregnancies,' she said wryly. 'One moment, I will get him for you.' She flicked some switches on the telephone console and spoke rapidly into the receiver. Cass wondered briefly why she hadn't simply paged

Benito on the intercom, but her head was beginning to throb and all that mattered was persuading Benito to take her to the *hacienda* to collect the rest of her things, and then to the airport.

Luisa replaced the receiver and pressed the switch which unlocked the security door. Benito hurried out, his round face alight if slightly pink.

'Is very great pleasure to see you.' He pumped her hand and she felt his friendliness warm her like spring sunshine after a cold hard winter. He picked up her suitcase and indicated the open door. 'Please you come.'

'I'm sorry to descend on you like this without warning,' Cass apologised. 'It—well—plans were changed rather suddenly.'

'No trouble. Is OK, I promise. You like some coffee?' He opened the door into his office and dropping her case, indicated a chair beside the filing cabinet. 'You sit, make comfortable. I fetch coffee.' He started out again.

'Benito,' Cass made to follow him, her anxiety growing. 'Please don't bother.' Sooner or later Miguel would reason that Benito was her only other contact in Mexico. She had to be gone by then. It wasn't fair to complicate Benito's life with her problems.

'Is no bother. I go quick. Back very soon. Please you sit. We talk later. Lots of time.' He closed the door firmly.

Cass stood in the middle of the room, assailed by doubts. She closed her eyes, rubbing her temples against the nagging ache. How kind Benito was, inviting her in as though he had nothing else to do. She was suddenly still. *He had not been surprised to see her.* Nor had Luisa. They had *expected* her. Which could only mean . . .

'Oh, no,' she whispered, and running to the door, snatched it open. 'Ben——' she started to call but the word choked off as she collided with a tall, black-haired figure clad in denim jeans and a pale blue roll-neck sweater of fine wool.

'No!' she gasped and turned to flee, but one strong brown hand snaked out and seizing her neck, thrust her back into Benito's office and slammed the door shut.

In one brief second of coherent thought Cass prayed for strength. Her pride was all she had left and she clung to it like a shield. But before she could utter a word he grasped her shoulders, glaring at her, his face a mask of cold fury.

'How dare you sneak from my house like a thief in the night!' She had never heard him so angry.

She had to swallow before she could speak. 'What difference does it make? Under the circumstances I could not stay.'

'*Who* said you could not stay? It is *my* house. Did *I* ask you to leave?' he shot back.

'No.' Cass shook her head wearily. 'I know it was perhaps less than polite to slip away as I did, but for pity's sake, Miguel,' she raised pain-filled eyes to his, 'can't you see, I simply couldn't take any more.' She forced a wry smile that suddenly faltered. 'Put it down to a clash of personalities.'

'You will not leave me,' his tone was ominous. 'I will not let you go.'

Ice-water trickled down her spine but she held her voice steady. 'You have no choice, Miguel.' Surely he must see that. Why was he making it so hard for them both? 'I came to ask Benito to take me to the *hacienda* to collect the rest of my things, and then to the airport.'

'No,' he said flatly.

'In God's name, Miguel,' Cass cried in anguish, 'what more do you want of me?'

'I told you,' he said softly, 'everything.'

Cass was filled with an incoherent rage. 'Go to hell, Miguel Ibarra! I am not a novelty you can play with then toss aside for a more familiar toy. You are going to marry

Teresa. I wish you both well, but I have other things to do.'

A fleeting expression crossed his face, then the deep frown lines that had trenched his forehead disappeared and a gleam appeared in his eyes. '*Who* said I am going to marry Teresa?' he enquired pleasantly.

'That is not very amusing, Miguel,' Cass snapped. 'I heard you—we all heard—last night. You and Don Diego——'

He rested his hands on his hips. 'You heard me say that it was time the matter was settled. It is settled. I am not going to marry Teresa.'

Cass was stunned. 'But she thought—everyone thought——'

He made an impatient gesture. 'I should not have permitted the charade to continue for so long. The betrothal was arranged between our families when Teresa was eighteen. It suited me to have a permanent partner for social occasions.'

Cass stared at him. 'Was that all it meant to you?'

He shrugged. 'It was useful for extricating myself from affairs which became too demanding.' His cold arrogance shook her but she recognised his total honesty.

'And Teresa? What about her?'

His smile was grim and humourless. 'Teresa cares for no one but Teresa. She was a spoilt child. She is now, despite considerable effort on my part to broaden her outlook, a selfish, petulant woman. When she grows up, if she ever does, she will make some wealthy man very happy, provided he seeks neither intellectual stimulation nor emotional support. She and Prentice deserve one another.'

Cass's eyes widened.

'I am not blind, Cassandra,' he said softly. 'And Prentice is not the first.' He looked deep into her eyes and her heart began to thump unevenly. She moistened her lips.

'Does she know yet?'

He nodded, his expression grim. 'It was not a scene I would wish to repeat. However, Don Diego proved most helpful.'

'*Helpful?*' Cass was bewildered. 'Feeling as he does about his daughter I'd have thought he'd be furious, threatening breach of promise and swearing vengeance.'

Miguel's dark brows slanted and one corner of his mouth lifted cynically. 'Ah, but feeling as he does about his business, gratitude overcame indignation.'

Totally nonplussed, Cass shook her head. 'What are you talking about?'

'I've bought his company,' Miguel replied.

'*You* have?' Cass gasped. 'But *why*? What do you want with a textile company?'

'Nothing.' He thrust his hands into the pockets of his jeans. 'But that was the price of my freedom.' His mouth twisted ironically. 'As soon as he heard that I would keep him on the board, Diego accepted the deal without argument or reservation.' He stared down at her, deep lines bracketing his mouth. 'Had I not met you I would probably have married Teresa. One of us would have been happy. She and her family were prepared to *overlook* my mixed ancestry in view of my wealth and position.' Beneath the dry irony, Cass sensed a thread of bitterness, and anger flared at the stupidity of people who were too insular and petty to recognise that it was the potent mixture of genes, his links with the past, that made him the man he was. But he was not seeking her sympathy, nor would he appreciate it, proud devil that he was, so she bit her lip and kept silent.

'But after you had ridden with me into the hills and we watched the sun rise together, I knew marriage to Teresa was impossible.' He took a step forward and caught her shoulders, his expression almost angry. 'You were the woman I wanted.'

Cass's eyes flew wide and her breath caught in a tiny hiss. His voice was rough and harsh. 'We knew each other, you and I. So much said, recognised, without words. I was afraid to believe in you. You could not be all you seemed. I had to probe, to test. I hurt you, I despised myself.'

Recalling his remark about Mexicans rarely divulging their true feelings, Cass began to realise just how difficult it was for him to reveal his confusion. All the love she had fought so hard to control welled up and overflowed, filling her with such joy she could hardly breathe.

'Oh, Miguel,' she whispered, reaching up with infinite tenderness to caress the blunt, square line of his jaw. He had not shaved and her fingers rasped against the dark stubble. 'Do I mean so much to you?' A thousand tiny flames flickered along her nerve ends as his hands, hard and possessive, slid down her back to draw her close.

'You are life to me,' he rasped. 'I could say nothing of my feelings while I was still betrothed to Teresa. And it was wrong of me to make love to you but,' his arms tightened and she felt, in the tense hardness of his body, his need for her, '*Dios*, I am flesh and blood, not stone!' He threaded his fingers through her hair and tugged gently, forcing her head back, exploring her face with a hunger that made her dizzy.

'H-how did you know I'd come here?' Cass could scarcely believe what she was hearing. It was a mirror image of all *she* had been through.

'How else could you get back to the *hacienda*?' He smiled. 'The helicopter has never flown so fast. I arrived here only minutes before you.' He lifted one hand, imprisoning her chin between his fingers and thumbs.

'I came to your room early, as soon as I had spoken with Teresa. I wanted to tell you I was free, to ask you to fly to Texas with me to meet my parents. But you had gone, leaving that cruel note.'

'Cruel?' Cass repeated, shaken. 'All it said was that I wished you well.'

His mouth tightened. 'How could you wish me well and yet run away?' he demanded harshly. 'You knew how I felt about you.'

'No.' She shook her head, wrenching her chin free. 'I knew how *I* felt and I could not stay and watch you marry someone else.'

'But I had no intention of marrying anyone else.' His voice rose in frustration.

'*I* didn't know that,' Cass cried. 'You hadn't seen fit to tell me!'

'Do you love me?' he demanded. His dark gaze pierced her very soul.

'Do you need to ask?' she whispered.

His eyes were suddenly vulnerable. 'I need to be told,' he said quietly.

Cass smoothed the thick, springy hair back from his temples, glorying in its texture, in the warmth of his bronze skin. 'I love you, Miguel. I loved you almost from that first moment, though I did not recognise it, and I will love you until I die.' She would have said more, but his mouth stopped her.

It started as a gentle kiss, tender and cherishing, a solemn pledge to their future together. But after a few moments as his breathing quickened, his mouth grew more demanding. His hand caressed her hair, her throat, then moved down to cup her breast. Cass clung to him, giving as he gave, taking as he took, engulfed by the swirling torrent of passion.

At last he broke free, holding her, limp and trembling, away from him. His breathing was ragged, his eyes aflame. 'We will marry soon, *very* soon,' he announced. 'Do you have any family you wish to be present? I will fly them out.'

Cass shook her head. 'My parents are both dead. I have some distant cousins, but no one close.' She felt a momentary pang.

Miguel put his arm around her. 'Then my family will be yours. They will love and cherish you as I do.' Touched by his gentleness and understanding, Cass's eyes filled with tears. 'Come,' he drew her towards him, 'let us go home.'

She glanced up at him, the question in her eyes.

'The *hacienda* is *my* home,' he smiled. 'The house at San Miguel belongs to my parents. We visit each other quite often. My father likes to keep his finger on the pulse of our small empire.' He grimaced and Cass recognised the love and respect beneath his gentle mockery. She sighed softly.

'What is it, *querida*? Are you tired?'

'A little, but it's not that. I was just thinking about Derek.'

Miguel's features hardened, becoming all planes and angles. 'What about him?'

'Don't look like that.' She smiled up at him. 'Miguel, what are you going to do about the contract?'

'What contract?'

'The deal Derek said he came out here to arrange. The purchase of gemstones from Ibarra mines.'

'There will be no contract,' Miguel said coldly, looking down his nose at her. 'I will have no business dealings with thieves.'

'But he didn't——' Cass began.

'He tried to,' Miguel interrupted. 'You know it and I know it.' Cass lowered her eyes as he went on. 'The safe has electric eyes and sensor beams which I must deactivate every time I reach into it. Prentice did not know that.'

Cass's face mirrored her shock. 'Then it wasn't an accident.'

Miguel shook his head with slow deliberation.

'But why?' she whispered. '*Why* would he do such a thing? It doesn't make sense.'

Miguel shrugged. 'Like Teresa, Prentice is a spoilt child who never grew up. His drinking is a measure of his immaturity. He sensed something between you and me and was jealous. He wanted to hit back. To steal from me would have given him a sense of power. He is not a man, *querida*. He has cunning but little intelligence. He has grand ideas but no integrity. Naturally you will resign from the Prentice company.'

'That won't be necessary.' She pulled a wry face. 'He's already sacked me. It doesn't matter,' she touched his arm as his expression darkened, 'I'm just so sorry for his father. Matthew Prentice was very good to me.'

He stared at her thoughtfully. 'Then for that reason alone I will not press charges against him. He may stay on at San Miguel with the Moreloses until we return from Texas.' A smile softened his haughty features. 'The doctors say my father is making good progress. He is demanding to come home.'

Cass put her arms around him. 'Oh, Miguel, that's marvellous. If you have to come back for business, perhaps I can stay on with your mother just for a day or two. She may be glad of my company. The last few days must have been a terrible strain for her.'

Miguel crushed her to him. '*Dios*, but I love you so much.' He released her suddenly and lifting her left hand, kissed her third finger. 'One moment.' He fumbled in his pocket then slid a ring on to her finger. 'Perfect.' There was a satisfied smile in his voice.

Cass blinked and gasped. The magnificent fire opal.

blazed from a frame of tiny blue-white diamonds, their brilliance a perfect setting for the crimson stone with its shimmering fiery heart. 'Oh! It's *beautiful*! But how—you said——'

'—I knew the owner and that no amount of money would persuade him to sell.' He raised her hand and touched his lips to the ring. 'The stone was mine, *querida*, and now it is yours, as I am.'

Her face was luminous. 'Let's go home, Miguel,' she whispered.

As Benito and Luisa drank a toast in cold coffee and the helicopter flew eastward, high above the rolling hills an eagle dipped and soared, spiralling slowly skyward and out of sight.

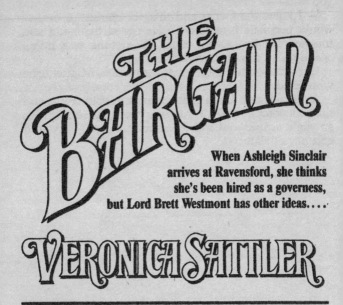

Six exciting series for you every month... from Harlequin

Harlequin Romance·
The series that started it all

Tender, captivating and heartwarming...
love stories that sweep you off to faraway places
and delight you with the magic of love.

♦

Harlequin Presents·

Powerful contemporary love stories...as individual as the women who read them

The No. 1 romance series...
exciting love stories for you, the woman of today...
a rare blend of passion and dramatic realism.

♦

Harlequin Superromance®
It's more than romance... it's Harlequin Superromance

A sophisticated, contemporary romance-fiction
series, providing you with a longer,
more involving read...a richer mix of complex plots,
realism and adventure.

Harlequin American Romance

Harlequin celebrates the American woman...

...by offering you romance stories written about American women, by American women for American women. This series offers you contemporary romances uniquely North American in flavor and appeal.

◆

Harlequin Temptation

Passionate stories for today's woman

An exciting series of sensual, mature stories of love...dilemmas, choices, resolutions... all contemporary issues dealt with in a true-to-life fashion by some of your favorite authors.

◆

Harlequin Intrigue

Because romance can be quite an adventure

Harlequin Intrigue, an innovative series that blends the romance you expect... with the unexpected. Each story has an added element of intrigue that provides a new twist to the Harlequin tradition of romance excellence.

Harlequin Books

PROD-A-2

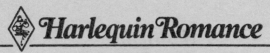

Harlequin Romance

Coming Next Month

Available in December wherever paperback books are sold,
or through Harlequin Reader Service.

In the U.S.
901 Fuhrmann Blvd.
P.O. Box 1397
Buffalo, N.Y. 14240-1397

In Canada
P.O. Box 603
Fort Erie, Ontario
L2A 5X3